The pain of her mother's disappearance has marked Rosamund's life...

"After the wedding there was a party," Rosamund explained. "Nurse gave me a piece of fruitcake and some hot cider. The cake was so delicious that I sneaked a second piece. Nurse came just then to take me away to get ready for bed. I didn't want her to know I had taken more cake so I hid my hand behind my back. The cake stained my new frock and she scolded me for being greedy. She said God would punish me. I felt so ashamed that I cried myself to sleep." Rosamund pressed her fingers to her lips, as if the memory was still painful.

"Later I was told the guests had played games after I went to bed. During hide-and-seek, my mother went to hide. Several guests saw her go down the hall toward the chapel." She stopped.

"Yes?" Eric prompted softly.

"That was the last anyone ever saw her. Everyone searched, but nobody found her—and she never came back. Ever."

Tears glistened on her lashes as she went on to confide her inmost childhood fear. "I thought it was my fault—that God was punishing me." She hesitated, considering, and then confided, "Papa blamed God. He's ignored God ever since." The suspended tears spilled down her cheeks, and she quickly reached up to whisk them away.

JOYCE WILLIAMS lives in Washington State where she is very active in her church and women's groups, and she has written several articles. Joyce was encouraged by the ladies in the various congregations her husband has pastored to strive to have her first book published.

The Lady Rose

Joyce Williams

Heartsong Presents

*To my husband Paul, who believed in me,
and to my children, Devorah, Rachel, and Timothy,
who gave up time with me so I could pursue my
dream. Thank you.*

A note from the author:
*I love to hear from my readers! You may write to me at
the following address:*   **Joyce Williams
Author Relations
P.O. Box 719
Uhrichsville, OH 44683**

ISBN 1-57748-150-X

THE LADY ROSE

Cover illustration by Chris Cocozza.

PRINTED IN THE U S A

Author's Note

Recorded in my family's history book which my grandfather Alfred Leopold Brandt translated from German into English, is the account of a Swedish commander who marched his troops across the frozen Baltic Sea to come to the aid of a European feudal lord under threat of attack by a neighboring landowner. In the ensuing battle, led by the Swedish commander, the enemy was defeated and his fortress was burned (Brandt means "one who took a fortress and burned it"). The Swedish commander married the daughter (an only child) of the feudal lord. The Swedish commander was my ancestor. The Brandt family remained in northern Europe until 1913 when my grandfather and his brothers came to America.

Stimulated to do some research, I discovered that the Baltic Sea did, in fact, freeze solid only once in recorded history: the winter of 1422–23. "What's Happening to Our Climate?" in the November 1976 issue of *National Geographic* documents this unusual phenomenon and refers to this period in history as "The Little Ice Age."

As a child I heard many stories told by my grandfather about his homeland and past. One of those stories was the gripping account of a lady who disappeared at a wedding; her fate was not discovered until many years later. I set out to combine historical facts with this unforgettable tale. The result is *The Lady Rose*.

one

In utter abandon, her long dark hair streaming behind her and the wind snatching at her breath, Rosamund Schmidden gave Pfeiffer his head. Horse and maiden, they galloped together as one. They were sensitive, spirited, loyal—friends since that first day when he had stood still for her to mount. He had watched her grow up. And now she was no longer a child.

Fair-skinned with masses of thick dark curling hair that waved away from a widow's peak and framed her oval face, sixteen-year-old Rosamund was the mirror of her English-born mother. High cheekbones, blue eyes that could dance with a streak of mischief, and a perfectly straight little nose gave her a classic beauty that wouldn't fade with age. Her chin was a bit on the determined side, but smiling lips and the lilt in her voice communicated a warm and friendly nature.

A white star rested in the center of Pfeiffer's forehead, and his satiny coat and silky mane shone blue-black in the afternoon sunshine. The path Rosamund chose for them wound its way through the fertile valley and played follow-the-leader with the river. Fallen autumn leaves covered the landscape, and in symmetrical row after row, the quiet fields extended from the pathway. Dense woods covered the not-too-distant hills, and a blanket of snow lay on the majestic mountain peaks backed against the horizon.

There were no clouds in the sky and the setting sun smiled an illusion of warmth from over the far southeastern ridges. Rosamund took a deep breath of crisp air; tomorrow it might be winter, but for this day it was still autumn.

Lately, a jaunt down the twisting descent and across the decaying countryside had become a daily affair. Faces tingling, Rosamund and Pfeiffer plunged headlong into the crisp air, leaving steamy vapor from their breath to shiver and shimmer behind them. Rosamund drank in the frosty air until her lungs ached and her recent worries were immobilized, chilled into silence— worries about Papa's health and peace of mind. For a few brief moments the countryside blurred, and reality became a muted shadow. But, like always, the illusion faded just when it seemed they could go on forever.

On this day, it was the echoing "Gong! Gong!" of the tower bell announcing dinner that called them back from their brief reprieve. Even as Rosamund reluctantly slowed Pfeiffer to a trot and turned him around, reality settled down on her like a cloak, and her heart once again weighed heavy with foreboding.

At the base of the outcropping she reigned in, and Pfeiffer began the challenging climb back up to Burg Mosel, the imposing castle at the summit. It stood as a bastion of security to the many villages dotting the countryside below. The bell in the central tower regularly announced mealtimes, and the imposing keep looked down its noble nose on the surrounding countryside.

Inside the walls, a cobbled drive passed along the front of the castle and stretched around to the stables at the

back. Sixteen grand stone steps led up to the front
entrance. Flower-filled jardinieres sat on the stone corners of the balustrade on either side of a central fountain.
Massive double doors, ornately carved and faced with
worked iron that reinforced their strength were beautiful
as well as intimidating.

Above the entrance two guardian angels were carved
into the stone, their impassive faces never revealing that
they kept watch over all who arrived and departed.
Arching shuttered windows wrapped around the grand
manor on three levels like holiday garland, and a blue
flag flew proudly from the pinnacle of the highest-
reaching tower. An awesome sight, it heralded "All is
well!" to everyone who looked up to it for assurance.
Sadly, Rosamund wished for herself and Papa the peace
her home represented to so many others.

ɷ

Inside the stately residence, the silence of the great
room was disturbed only by the snapping of a fire and
the restless shifting of a pair of oversized feet in leather
boots, extensions of the powerful figure sitting in a
large, heavily carved oak chair. The man's massive
hands gripped the broad chair arms and his fingers
clenched and unclenched almost rhythmically. His
heavy brows were drawn low over deep-set eyes and
anxious lines creased his face where smile wrinkles usually rested.

Lost in thought, Lord Nicklaus Schmidden stared into
the fire. Through the years sorrow had been his constant,
suppressed companion. Now, however, the exposed
nerve felt rubbed too raw to be disguised, and he sighed
often—deep painful breaths that seemed to drain his

heart. Sometimes he thought talking to someone would relieve the steady throb of anxiety, but the question always was, "To whom?"

He couldn't confide in the servants; they would be filled with fear. Curtis, his clerk? No. No point in worrying him. And Rosamund—well, how could he tell his daughter that their arrogant, neighboring estate owner, Lord Frederick, had demanded her hand in marriage and threatened a full-scale attack if he refused? No, Rosamund must not be told; she might consider it her duty to sacrifice herself for his sake. Yet if he refused Lord Frederick's demands, he could very possibly lose his daughter anyway!

His brows met as his frown deepened. He gripped the chair arms until the veins stood out like cords on the backs of his large hands. There must be some pathway leading out of this dilemma back to peace of mind, peace of heart, peace of home. He knew there had to be a way—if he could just find it.

"I must!" he insisted aloud, pounding a clenched fist on the broad arm of his sturdy chair. His resolution bounced off the stone walls, echoing like the relentless thoughts that pounded the halls of his troubled mind. Then slowly the echoes faded back into sullen silence.

~

Rosamund slipped into the great room, rosy-cheeked and glowing from the fresh air. As she looked around, a shadow crossed her face. Almost, she thought she had heard conversation, as though words had fallen to the marble floor and were waiting to be picked up. Following a puzzled glance at her father, who sat staring into space, she ran her long, slim fingers through her tangled curls and smoothed the skirt of her rumpled brown riding frock. Following another quick look at her father, she pulled a stool close to the fire and bent low to sit on it. As graceful as a willow bough, she leaned toward the blaze and stretched out her slender hands to its comforting warmth.

The fire provided a backdrop of light for her delicate silhouette and her movements near the hearth snagged her father's attention. Startled by the picture she made, sculpted by the flames, Lord Schmidden saw in his mind another Rose—with just such curling hair, patrician features, and long, expressive fingers. He clenched his teeth as the old pain of his loss stabbed like a knife. He had already lost one Rose; he had no intention of losing the other.

Rosamund turned at his sigh. "What's the matter, Papa? Are you worried about something?"

He got to his feet, laid his large hand tenderly on the top of her dark head, and replied, "Everything is fine, dear. There's no need to be fretting yourself about me." His broad thumb smoothed her brow, his light touch erasing the furrows. Oh, how he wished he could push back the years as easily as he wiped away her frown. Why, oh, why did little girls have to grow up?

He turned away and hurried out of the room. In the corridor he paused and passed his hand over his face— as if he could erase the thoughts behind it.

෴

Rosamund bit back the questions she longed to ask. She knew her father was troubled, more troubled than she had ever seen him. The tension seemed to increase from day to day.

She shifted on the stool to look up at the likeness of her mother hanging above the fireplace. Wistfully, she tried to remember her, but the memories, like the canvas itself, were faded. She remembered bedtime stories. Walks in the garden. The scent of perfume. Glittering earrings. And the feel of a velvety skirt against her cheek. Memories as soft and distant as an elusive scent.

"Oh, Mama," she addressed the face in the canvas, "what would you have said to Papa?" She shook her head in dismay. Poor, dear Papa. This was not the first time she had made an attempt to share his problems. And just like each time before, he had hastily escaped the conversation. What could possibly be causing him such distress? Why wouldn't he talk to her about it?

Invincible, Papa had always been. Wise and gentle and doting. None of her girlish troubles had confounded him. He could right each wrong and kiss away every fear. And when she had missed the guidance of a mother, he had sat her on his knee and gentled her through the bewildering dilemmas of adolescence. He adored her, and she delighted in pleasing him. But recently he had been distracted, preoccupied, and she felt like a child again, protected—but left out.

Her puzzled thoughts were called back by the sound of her father's heavy footsteps on the stone floor in the next room. She stood up, drew in a long breath, and went quickly down the hall.

The wide doors of the magnificent dining room stood open, and candlelight flickered on the glass panes in the header windows above the doors, windows that could be opened in summer to provide a breeze. Rosamund paused in the doorway for a moment, noting that the long refectory table was set for two at one end. The table's solid legs ended in clawed feet, and vines were etched into the outer rim of its inlaid top that now glimmered in the firelight.

Rich-hued woven Flemish tapestries hung on several walls, and shutters and draperies cloaked the recessed windows. Dark paneling concealed the stone walls, and ornate moldings framed the high ceiling frescoed with long-faced saints and plump cherubs. The glow cast by the candles burning in the sixteen-arm chandelier suspended over the table colored everything a rosy amber.

Her father, arms locked over his chest, stood staring blankly at the ornate-handled swords—swords wielded by his great-grandfather when gaining possession of Schmidden territory—that were mounted to the left of the fireplace. His shoulders were hunched and his face, chiseled by shadows, betrayed his fear: fear that he might lose his inheritance—property that was the essence of his identity—and his daughter—his purpose for living.

Mustering her courage, Rosamund came close and laid her hand on his arm. "Papa," she appealed, "please tell me what's wrong. You've been worrying for days— I know you have! Maybe if you'd tell me why, I could help."

He turned to look at her with startled eyes. "Oh, Rosamund, I didn't mean for you to know."

She tugged at his arm with both hands, "Know what, Papa?"

Her father remained silent for a long time and finally he sighed, "Your mother. . ." He stopped abruptly.

She waited, hoping he would finish his sentence. But he didn't. He never did. Instead, he took a deep breath and said matter-of-factly, "Our property is bordered by the Baltic Sea on the north and other landowners surround us inland. We have more land than any other lord. We've all lived as peaceful neighbors for nearly a hundred years.

"But recently there's been quarreling between two villages, one on either side of our border with Lord Frederick. Raiding parties have repeatedly attacked us, and the situation continues to get worse. I've tried to make peace—why, I even offered restitution for *their* losses! But Lord Frederick has demanded. . ."

He nervously pinched his lower lip. "Lord Frederick has threatened to unite the neighboring estates against me. If he succeeds. . ." Rosamund's father grimaced, raising his brows and shaking his head. "We're not strong enough to fend off all of them."

He rubbed his throbbing temples with his broad fingertips and stared at the floor. Then, as though speaking to himself, he continued, "Winter will buy me some time, but by early spring I've got to have help."

His voice had faded to a harsh whisper as he reluctantly admitted his vulnerability. His big hands dropped to Rosamund's slender shoulders, and he gave her a little shake. "I turned my back on God when your mother disappeared. . ." Again his agonized words trailed off into painful silence.

At last, drawing in a ragged breath, he finished, "I told God to get out of my life, and I forbade anyone to mention Him. I took it upon myself to take care of all the families living on our land, to make the land prosperous, and to make you happy." His words were sharp and clipped with a bitter twist. "But now God has me in a corner." His hands fell to his sides, and he groaned as he turned away.

The sounds of servants entering the room with dinner shattered the intensity of the moment. Lord Schmidden instantly recovered his composure. Rosamund swallowed her words. Only her eyes revealed her dismay.

શ

Burg Mosel lay deathly still, pinioned on its lofty mount. No moonlight softened its corners and peaks. No wind blew away the ghastly pall that pressed in upon it. And inside, the embers flickered fretfully as the huge fire in the hearth of the great room burned itself out. Rosamund's little stool sat empty. The decanters on the sideboard had given up their last drops. Lone, solitary, disconsolate, Lord Schmidden slumped in his massive chair.

The burning torment of frustration had passed. Instead, black despair shrouded him like a hooded robe of mourning, and all that remained of his hopes were the corpses of discarded ideas, each one cast aside into a shallow grave along the downward spiral of defeat. How long he had sat there brooding, he didn't know. Grief isn't measured in time.

Into this deadly silence came the uncanny awareness of another's presence. It flickered. It beckoned. Was it just a shadow—or perhaps a moonbeam? Maybe it was the dawn. Maybe it was. . .God. He couldn't be certain, but he had nowhere else to turn. He spoke tentatively. Fearfully. "God, is that You?" He directed his hesitant, hopeful question at the faintly glowing embers, desperation at last overruling his long-nursed pride.

Even as he stared into the silent fireplace, he heard the voice of a dying log as it shifted. The charred coals burst once again into brilliant flames, sending him a message like Moses' burning bush. In that instant of revelation, Lord Schmidden came straight out of his chair. Oh, yes! He didn't know how he knew, but he knew: God had heard him. And he knew with certainty that God had a plan!

two

It was midmorning, and already the dank basement scullery steamed with odors of soured food and sweat. Rosamund perched on a three-legged stool. Although her position in life would have dictated otherwise, she spent her free time with the servants who had been a part of her life for as long as she could remember.

The scullery was her favorite haunt, particularly because Kathe, one of the scullery maids, was close in age to her mistress. In contrast to Rosamund's slender grace, Kathe's angular figure was sturdy and accustomed to hard work. Her brown hair fell in a single braid down her back. She had merry brown eyes, a wide smile, and a cheerful disposition that made her everyone's friend. At Rosamund's insistence Kathe had received a minimal education. She was often included in Rosamund's lessons when Kathe's mother would allow it.

Kathe's mother, Hildy Stone, was manager of the scullery. She was tall and spare, and strong bones stood out in her thin face. Strands of gray hair escaped the severe knot at the back of her neck. Her mouth was large, and her smile lit her whole face.

Quite aware of the danger of giving Kathe more options than her station in life afforded, Hildy nevertheless saw herself in her daughter, and her own longing for more from life than the four walls of the scullery with its dirty plates, dishes, and cooking utensils overruled her social judgment. She allowed her daughter's friendship with the lady of the house to develop. Not that she permitted Kathe to shirk her duties; quite to the contrary, to ease her conscience, Hildy worked Kathe harder than the other maids. Frequently, Rosamund helped Kathe with her work so the two of them could have time to slip outside the castle wall for a walk, to pick wildflowers or berries, or to play girlish games—and the two of them spent many happy hours together. Rosamund borrowed homespun frocks from Kathe for such adventures, drawing the eyelet laces that ran down the back as tightly as possible to make them fit her more slender figure. In this way her own lovely gowns, provided by Papa with great pride, remained fresh and beautiful.

As she wiped dry the last of the breakfast crockery, Rosamund frowned at thoughts of Lord Frederick's threat and her own scanty knowledge of their neighboring landowner.

The Schmiddens had two fortified residences, which they occupied seasonally. When food supplies were low and the lavatories and moat were foul, the household would move to another residence. A number of servants would remain behind to dredge the moat, clean the living quarters, and restock the castle with supplies.

Rosamund and her father spent the warm summer months at Feste Burg, a fortress built nearly two hundred years earlier. The weathered stone and mortar fortress, its turrets and towers resembling inverted sugar cones, perched on a craggy cliff. The tallest tower had been designed as a lookout to detect sea invaders. However, Feste Burg had not seen threatening action against it since before the birth of the present Lord Schmidden, and for Rosamund, while summers at Feste Burg meant few household luxuries, there were many happy hours roaming up and down the nearby seacoast, usually with Pfeiffer for companionship, that compensated for the inconveniences.

In contrast to Feste Burg, the Schmiddens' primary residence, Burg Mosel, stood near the southern inland boundary of their property. It was an elegant, palatial castle, with wide window arcades, an ornate interior, and spacious rooms that could accommodate gracious entertaining. When Lord Schmidden had been a boy, tournaments, games, and hunts were exciting social events, and on special occasions guests enjoyed the talents of a band of minstrels or a harpist.

Located on a lofty ridge a half-day's journey by horse from Burg Mosel, Lord Frederick's fortress had recently been completed. This formidable fortress boasted a large cylindrical keep and the newly popularized *en bosse* exterior—according to servant gossip.

At this point in her musing, Rosamund betrayed her anxiety with giddy conversation. "Kathe, did you ever tell your mother about the day we met Lord Frederick?" The words were as glossy as silk and rich with undertones.

Kathe darted a quick, apprehensive glance at her mother. "Why, no," her voice rose, as though to imply such a thought had never occurred to her, the event being so unimportant.

Hildy, not wishing to reveal her curiosity, feigned disinterest; she averted her gaze and continued working as though the task at hand required her utmost attention.

Rosamund clasped her arms around one knee and cocked her head as if she expected it would help her remember. Blue eyes brimming with mischief, she baited, "Oh, Hildy! We did indeed meet the handsome Lord Frederick—and such a charming man you've never seen!"

"Ach! And how did this come to be?" Hildy deliberately allowed herself to be drawn into the discussion.

"I thought you'd never ask! It was last spring, several days before Papa and I left for Feste Burg, when Kathe and I went out for a walk. We picked a bouquet of wildflowers for you. Don't you remember?" Rosamund smiled audaciously and continued her teasing. "You had scolded Kathe earlier that day, so we brought you a peace offering."

A servant girl of twenty, Kathe had another year before she could legally marry without Lord Schmidden's arrangement or consent, but it was common knowledge that Curtis O'Donnell, Lord Schmidden's freckled, red-haired Gaelic clerk, was quite fond of the jolly scullery maid. Hildy was pleased and fiercely determined that nothing should interfere. Cloaking her fear in jest, she frequently threatened Kathe to a week in the dungeon with the rats for company if she expressed even a particle of interest in anyone beside Curtis.

Because of this, the girls took shameless delight in teasing her and had, on several occasions, deliberately led her to believe Kathe was interested in one of the local village youths.

Kathe joined the frivolous conversation. "Oh, Mother! We honestly forgot where we were in our search for flowers—"

"And we crossed over onto Lord Frederick's land," Rosamund finished the sentence. There was a naughty twinkle in her eye as she went on to explain, "Only we didn't *know* we were on his property."

Hildy stopped her scrubbing, standing with both arms buried nearly to the elbows in dirty dishwater. "You went that far alone!" The jesting was no longer funny.

Kathe avoided an answer. Hoping to make things better by getting on with the story, she said hastily, "We came to a clearing—we'd been in the woods to the south. Two men were stalking a deer. . ."

"Go on," Hildy prodded in a voice full of frown. Her large mouth drew into a straight line.

Rosamund lifted her chin, remembering. "Well, I thought they were poaching on Papa's land, so I shouted, 'What do you think you're doing?' " One dark eyebrow quirked up as she continued. "Of course I spooked the buck, and the two men came running toward us, shouting and angry. Kathe tried to pull me into the woods, but I shook her off. There wasn't anyone else to set them straight—so I didn't back down at all."

Not for the world would she admit she had been terrified.

"They glared at us. The short, squatty man was puffing —I'd guess he was about Papa's age, don't you think, Kathe? The other man was younger and tall with curly, dark hair and bold, black eyes. Oh, he was handsome." Rosamund rolled her eyes melodramatically and both girls giggled, embarrassed to acknowledge how much he attracted them. "Wickedly handsome!"

Hildy pursed her lips and prompted, "And then. . ." She dried her work-roughened hands on her skirt and turned to lean against the sturdy workbench.

"Well, so then I asked them why they were hunting on Lord Schmidden's property when that's his privilege. The short man snorted and asked who I thought I was, telling them what to do!" The words had tumbled out so quickly that Rosamund stopped to catch a breath before she went on. "The handsome man raised his black eyebrows and stared at me. Then he asked who was I, that I would be trying to protect Lord Schmidden's property all by myself!"

Kathe gave a short, nervous laugh. "Oh, Mother, you should have seen her! She got that indignant 'I beg your pardon' look on her face and said, 'I happen to be his daughter!' "

Pride and chagrin were mingled on Rosamund's face, and Hildy, eyes narrowed, stood silently alert. Innocence is a wonderful virtue, but flaunting it, even in ignorance, often costs dearly. Oh, how well she knew! She had paid for her own foolishness with a life of servitude and a fatherless child.

Kathe, seeing the alarm on her mother's face, rushed on. "Then they both burst out laughing. I guess they thought we were trying to bluff our way out of a sticky situation. Besides, Rosamund no more looked like Lord Schmidden's daughter than I did! Her hair had come loose, and she was wearing one of my old frocks."

Rosamund took up the story. "And then Lord Frederick said, 'Of course you're Lord Schmidden's daughter—and I'm the King of France!' and he winked at me like I was a foolish child."

"She blushed, and we all laughed," Kathe hastened to add, relief edging her voice.

"I did," Rosamund nodded, her color high, "but I was really glad they weren't still angry." Truth told, she was older and wiser for the experience. "So when Lord Frederick said we'd best be going back where we'd come from, we ran nearly all the way back to Burg Mosel!" Rosamund released her hold on her knee and sat up straight on the stool.

"Hmmm. . ." Hildy lowered her eyes to hide her thoughts. "How did you find out he was Lord Frederick?" She resumed her pot-scrubbing.

"When we got back here, I asked Curtis about our property boundaries and also if he'd ever met Lord Frederick. He described the landmarks. And he's met Lord Frederick twice." Rosamund paused before adding, almost as an afterthought, "I never did tell Papa, though."

"So why'd you think of it today?" Hildy eyed the young girl shrewdly.

"How should I know?" Rosamund exclaimed uncomfortably, nearly falling off the stool in her haste to get away. "Besides," the words floated back over her shoulder, "I really must be going." She hurried out the arched stone doorway and her rapid footsteps could be heard echoing in the stone stairwell.

When quietness had returned to the scullery, Hildy was heard to mutter under her breath, "There's hair in the soup! Miss Rosamund couldn't wait to get out of here." Her voice rose, "And Kathe, don't you ever. . ." Hildy proceeded to follow up the conversation with a few choice words directed toward her daughter.

❧

Making her way back up the dark flight of narrow steps to the main floor, Rosamund's fingers vibrated as she ran them along the cold stone walls—just like her thoughts vibrated intense pique. *I really thought Lord Frederick might call on Papa, if for no other reason than to find out if I was telling the truth. We might have been friends.*

There were so few men in her life who could be considered suitable marriage partners. As the only heir to the Schmidden property and all the responsibility which that entailed as protector for the many families living on their land, Rosamund knew she would have to marry someone capable of managing her affairs, with or without love. But her girlish heart couldn't help but dream.

Later that morning, Rosamund sought refuge in the music salon. Normally partitioned off from the great room by heavy draperies, the lovely room was suitable for a cozy *tête-à-tête* or secluded practice. However, the ell could be opened up to join the great room by swagging the curtains into ornate brass hooks on either side of the doorway. If the furnishings were pushed against the walls or temporarily removed to another location, a small group of musicians could easily fit with space to spare.

Originally used for storage, the room had been redefined by Rosamund's grandmother, Lady Clara Schmidden. Fond of parties, dramas, and musicales, Lady Clara had decided that the cobwebby storage room would make a perfect place for an orchestra. The remodeling had obviously been given much thought. The walls were faced with large rose-grained marble panels that were not only beautiful, but reflected sound as well. And the floor glowed with a mosaic sunburst. Imported from Italy, it had arrived in tiny pieces, and a skilled artisan had been brought in to lay it. The several months it had taken him proved time well spent; the end result was a breathtaking combination of intense lapis blue, sun yellow, grass green, and cherry red. The music salon was Rosamund's favorite room in the entire residence.

The harpsichord sat at the center of the sunburst. Lord Schmidden had purchased it for Rose soon after they were married. A young Frenchman, a traveling musician by the name of Pierre Monet, had been engaged to teach Rose to play, and he had remained in their employ for well over a year. However, following his decision to move on, he stopped in occasionally to visit, always ostensibly to check up on his former pupil.

Then, for two years following the mysterious disappearance of Lady Rose, the instrument was not played. But one day, when young Rosamund was just seven years old, her father had discovered her perched on the harpsichord's tall bench, picking out little melodies. Even though her legs were still too short to reach the floor, she eagerly tried to express the music she could hear in her head.

Her father had stood outside the curtains, listening. When at last he peeked in, he'd experienced a stab of bitter nostalgia at seeing anyone sitting in Rose's place, but the sensation passed in the next moment when Rosamund played the song she had composed. He kept her secret, slipping silently away. But when the time came to engage a new governess, he chose an older widow who played well and demonstrated a love for music.

Frau Meta recognized the inherent feel for music in her new charge and carefully fostered both lessons and love, knowing that anyone can play notes but not everyone can play music. Under her watchful tutelage Rosamund became quite accomplished. Music provided a constructive outlet for excess energy and outbursts of emotions, especially during the long lonely winter days when she had finished her lessons with Frau Meta, Kathe had more than enough work to keep her busy, and Papa was absorbed in overseeing the villages on his land or away on a trip to some foreign place.

On this day, Rosamund's slender fingers labored over the keys, agonizing through one melancholy piece after another. Her head drooped, and not a trace of her usual smile was to be seen. There had been no further opportunity to talk to her father about the despair he had disclosed the previous evening, and Rosamund released her frustration through her music.

Her father found her there, playing intently. He walked in, his heavy footsteps immediately capturing her attention. Her playing abruptly ended, and she looked up to greet him cheerlessly. "Well, Papa. What brings you here this time of day?"

For all the emotion he displayed, his desperate confession of the evening before might never have happened. He tweaked a curl that teased her cheek, smiled indulgently down on her as though oblivious to her dejection, and replied, "Came to see my best girl!"

"Oh Papa! You're so sweet." Contrite, she made herself smile.

"Seriously, I did come because I. . ." He cleared his throat. "Because I've got a plan to propose to you."

Rosamund eyed him speculatively. He sounded like his old self, assured and confident.

He softened the coming blow, "I know you won't like

it at first, I didn't myself—" He rushed the words. "But I know it's for the best. So please listen to your wise old Papa!"

Rosamund made a little face at him, wrinkling up her nose and then relaxing into a smile again. "All right, I'm listening." But her brows still arched apprehensively, and she laced and unlaced restless fingers in her lap.

"As I told you yesterday, Lord Frederick has threatened to attack me. I don't want you here if he carries out his threat. So here's my plan. I want you to go to stay with Edith, my old nurse. I'll get help to settle the situation with Lord Frederick, and then when it's safe, I'll come get you."

He kept his voice light, but Rosamund sensed the undercurrent of his anxiety. She was on her feet before he had finished speaking, a mutinous set to her determined chin. "Do you really think for a minute that I'll leave you?" Her voice broke, "Don't you *want* me here with you?" Her burning eyes searched his face.

"You know I want you here," he protested vigorously, "but I'll worry a lot less if I know you're safe." He swallowed hard, adding quietly, "I couldn't bear it if anything happened to you." He eyed her, waiting, trying to give her room to make the choice herself. He knew she would have far less difficulty living with the situation if she had a part in the decision.

Rosamund's face reflected her struggle. Her father was the thread that tied her whole life together. How could she ever *choose* to leave him? Still, she realized he had already faced this difficult decision. He had chosen to do what would be best—for her. Now she too must make a choice. Somehow it came to her that this decision was the final step of becoming an adult.

"I'll go—but just for you, Papa," came her reluctant whisper, and she bit her lips to keep back the tears that floated just behind her shaky self-control.

Her father reached out and squeezed her shoulder in grateful appreciation, attempting to say lightly, "It won't be forever, you know."

As if saying so would make it true!

"I'll see to the arrangements at once. The sooner the better." He departed, obviously relieved to have secured Rosamund's cooperation.

Rosamund sank down onto the bench. She had deliberately chosen to find her happiness in the happiness of her father, to love him more than she loved herself. She placed her fingers back into playing position, striking out at the keys in an impromptu piece that caused the harpsichord to shudder under her force and told without words what it had cost her to give Papa peace of mind.

⁂

Several weeks passed. Weeks of preparation. Edith Baer, Lord Schmidden's childhood nurse, had been contacted, careful arrangements had been made, and then, all too soon, Rosamund stood waiting in the entrance hall of Burg Mosel, ready to say farewell to her father.

One trunk containing the bare necessities for her survival stood by the massive doors. Looking around, she felt so young and insignificant, dwarfed as she was by the grandeur of the entrance hallway with its vaulted ceiling, polished marble floor, and central staircase.

The burning candles in silver sticks positioned along each side wall, that usually flickered so brightly, seemed to cast gloomy shadows on everything. The faces staring out from the canvases that hung on the walls between the doorways, normally sober anyhow, seemed to be positively glowering.

Rosamund shuddered, shrugged off the sense of doom, and took in a deep breath just before Papa came out from the great room. She had expected him to hurry up to her and swing her around in a big hug, his customary greeting and farewell. Instead, he entered slowly. In his hands he carried a small ornate box which he carefully placed on top of her waiting trunk. Turning, he reached for the bell cord near the doors. With a sharp tug, he summoned her ride.

In the next instant, Rosamund found herself gathered into a close embrace, her cheek against her father's chest. He hugged her tightly for a moment. Then holding her just far enough away for him to see her face, he whispered in a choked voice, "I'll miss you, Rosamund, but it means everything to me to know you're safe. Always remember who you are, but don't confide our situation to anyone. I'll come for you as soon as I can—hopefully by summer." He kissed her firmly on both cheeks.

Then turning quickly, as if to maintain control over his emotions, he explained about the small enameled box. "I'm sending this little chest with you for safekeeping. It belonged to your mama, and I've always intended to give it to you once you were no longer a child. It seems events have hurried that moment. If anything should happen. . ." His gruff voice could go no further.

The heavy doors swung open to reveal a broad view of the winter wonderland below. That she would be faring forth into such a vast expanse without Papa, feeling so alone, struck Rosamund with new force. She caught her lower lip between her teeth.

While Henry, the liveryman, put her trunk and the little chest on the floor of the carriage, Papa handed her in. Giving her one more swift kiss, he said good-bye. She turned to watch until he could no longer be seen. Although, truth told, her eyes were so clouded with tears she couldn't see him anyway.

three

The December sunlight filtered through the leafless tree branches like fingers of God, touching with fleeting warmth the frozen world it reached. The young man who lay propped on one elbow on the cold earth was included in that touch. Along the edge of his fur hood, his blond hair formed a halo around his face, and his ruddy cheeks and tanned skin glowed in the sunlight.

But the turmoil raging inside Eric Branden remained untouched by the sunny fingers of God. Indecision tossed him about like a small boat at the mercy of a raging east wind. How to answer Lord Schmidden's request for help—that summed up his dilemma.

It had only been five days since Eric and his crew had returned from a grueling expedition, and the men needed rest. Eric felt he had already stretched common sense to return to Sweden so late into the season. If that wasn't sufficient reason to say no, snow, a threat to travel of any kind, was long overdue. Furthermore, easterly winds would soon be ruling the Baltic Sea, and then no one would venture out until spring. And the last possibility, to set off on foot around the sea, would take far too long; he would get there more quickly by waiting for spring. In either case, he would almost certainly arrive too late to be of much help.

Lord Schmidden had provided food and shelter for Eric and his crew seven years before when easterly

Baltic winds had blown them off course and damaged a sail rigging. In return for the kindness, Eric had promised a return of the favor if Lord Schmidden should ever need it, and had the request come at any other time, the answer wouldn't have been given a second thought. Even though the thrill of the sea's challenge no longer gripped him as it once had, nevertheless he would certainly have gone immediately to help his friend.

For twelve years Eric had been one with the sea, a Viking in the truest sense. Contrary to their reputation, Vikings were not all marauding pirates. They were, in fact, the cross-pollinators of culture, carrying news, customs, and social change from one civilization to another. And although many of Eric's contemporaries had married and settled into agrarian societies, a few explorers still roamed the seas, restless and adventuresome. Such were Eric and his crew.

Now twenty-eight, Eric struggled with a deep ache, a longing deliberately repressed these many years by devotion to the mental and physical rigors of the sea: he desired a home and a family of his own. That longing had surfaced with increasing frequency during this last expedition. As he contemplated yet another expedition, the desire for someone of his own and a place of stability tightened around his heart like raw sisal cords.

Not that there hadn't been eligible—even willing—maidens in his life. With the help of his five sisters-in-law and the ever-busy village matchmaker, whom he vigorously avoided, he could have settled down long ago. Or he could have followed the lead of his fellow crew members, Olaf and Karl: each had brought back a bride met on an expedition.

But things were different for Eric. Although the State Church had provided rote religion, he had hungered for active truth and knowledge. This hunger had driven him to the sea in his youth. And when Svenn, a Norwegian fisherman, had explained the reality of communication with God through Jesus Christ, Eric had opened his heart and experienced spiritual birth. With that new life, there was also born in him a desire for a woman who could share his faith, not just his kitchen and his bed.

Never, with the demands of his many expeditions, had there been time to develop that kind of a relationship. So the yearning, hidden yet growing, ruptured into agony. Should he go—again? Should he relinquish hope for time with someone? Was God asking him to take up the cross of duty to a friendship? Did God understand how rootless and lonely he felt? Could God indeed be trusted with his future?

He knew he'd given his word. But the timing of Lord Schmidden's request, the distance around the sea, and Eric's own personal despair were factors which refused to release him to a decision. Eric argued both sides with himself until he dropped his head, exhausted from the struggle. To go back on his word was unthinkable; it violated the sanction of his conscience. Yet, unless he could walk on water. . .

His conscience pricked for even entertaining such a presumptuous thought, and he jumped to his feet. He slapped his mitted hands together and stomped his feet to restore circulation. Words of aggravation at such a foolish idea burst forth. "Fantasy isn't faith—*nobody* walks on water!"

four

The air smelled of snow, but the frozen ground was still bald. Trees held up naked arms as though begging for winter coats. Spires of smoke rose like prayers from the cluster of chimneyed dwellings, and the villagers, young and old, found the unusually barren winter the main focus of neighbor-to-neighbor conversation.

That is, everyone except shriveled old Edith Baer. Edith scurried about with scarcely suppressed excitement. She left her friends to shake their heads and whisper covertly that Edith wasn't the same woman they had known these many years. Did she have some ailment that was causing her to sip the medicinal spirits she urged on the village sick and weary? But Edith's berry wine still perched above her fireplace. And while it had been carefully lifted down from its roost just the day before, it had received only a quick dusting—the same treatment given to everything else in her humble home.

No. Mother Baer, as the villagers affectionately nicknamed Edith, was not suffering ill effects from some medicinal treatment. Rather, she had a secret in her basket; she had a guest! She knew that within a few days her guest would replace the unseasonable weather as the main topic of village gossip. And she knew she would enjoy every detail of the attention. But for the moment it was her own sweet elixir.

Edith and Rosamund had made a feast of root veg-
etable stew and heavy black bread. Darkness was falling,
and Edith, now bundled warmly from head to toe, turned
back from the open doorway. "Be back soon, I will. I
must be lookin' in on Frau Lanz and her young'ns. They
be abed with the croup. Be puttin' more wood on the
fire, iffen ye will. I'll be knockin' when I come so's ye
can enter me."

She heaved against the door until it shut and plodded
away in the direction of the cluster of village houses,
her plump figure bobbing.

Edith's house was the last of the two dozen or so wood
and stone structures huddled together just where the
coastline reached out to form a bay that was sheltered
from sea winds. The small northern European village
nestled into the verdant lowland which extended down
to the coast where a row of mooring posts stuck up like
protruding hairpins.

When the door had shut out Edith and the cold, Rosamund looked around in dismay. Could it be that she was
actually here, in Edith's earthy little cottage? Dressed in
one of Kathe's homespun frocks that she had borrowed to
help disguise her noble identity, Rosamund Schmidden
sat on the rude bench that offered the room's only seat-
ing, thinking surely if she pinched herself she would
wake up from this frightful nightmare! But no. She was
awake—regrettably so. The humble dwelling had its own
peculiar personality. The lower walls, made up of brown
and gray stones that had been stuck together with gray
mortar, showed signs of disintegration here and there.
Fine gray powder had sifted to the floor, leaving empty
hollows behind, and the resulting silt rested in mounds

like miniature mountains around the bottom edges of the walls. Wooden beams formed the upper walls, dried mud with bits of straw poking out of it chinked in the cracks, and the hard-packed dirt floor had been scraped so many times that it was now a step lower than the door sill.

Rosamund groaned dispiritedly as she continued the appraisal of her shelter. The fireplace looked as if it had grown up right out of one of the lower stone walls. A diverse assortment of small bottles and crocks sat on the ledges made by the oddly shaped stones that stuck out from the face of the fireplace. On the left wall, random wooden pegs held several faded garments, a large basket, and three pails. A bed of straw filled in the corner on the floor along the right wall. Two comforters covered the straw, and Rosamund shuddered at just the thought of sleeping on the floor.

What if there were mice—or rats? Even Feste Burg, her family's summer residence, for all its spartan primitiveness, was furnished with bed frames that suspended sleepers off the floor. She swallowed a sob. She supposed she should be thankful there were no chickens or goats in Edith's house!

The firelight played peekaboo on the rafters, drawing her attention to the bundles of weeds that hung from the rough ceiling beams. Rolling her eyes, Rosamund straightened up from a disgruntled slouch. The crude bench rocked back and forth unsteadily, and she picked up one end and scooted it forward, but her effort made no difference. Shrugging her shoulders in resignation, she got up and put another log on the fire.

Staring into the flames, she thought again about saying good-bye to her father. Tears came to her eyes and she reached up to brush them away. The past several days had been unsettling, and more than once she had reminded herself that she was here by her own choice—Papa needed to be sure she was safe.

Oh, why did growing up have to be so hard? Every decision had to be carefully considered. Impetuosity had to be tempered by consideration for others. Adventure had consequences. Sometimes she knew she could conquer the world. At other times she wished to climb up on her father's knee and be a child again, self-centered and heedless of responsibility.

She turned abruptly away from the fire and dropped to her knees beside the small, brightly enameled chest Papa had sent with her. Using a fingertip, she slowly traced the outlines of the jewel-toned figures on its top. A faraway look filled her eyes as she reached out and pressed the tiny button at the center front near the closure to release the spring that secured the top of the chest. This small ornate chest represented her mother in a tangible way.

Rosamund smoothed the purple velvet lining and sniffed at the faintly sweet musky smell that came from inside the chest. The door to the past opened for a fraction of a memory and her fingers trembled involuntarily.

She squeezed one hand tightly in the other, determinedly pressed her lips together, and then reached out to examine the tiny wooden box that lay loose on top of the chest's other contents. She turned the little box over and over, as though suddenly reluctant to disturb the past. So often she had wished she had known her mother—yet now she felt almost afraid of intimacy with the unknown. Steeling herself against her emotions, she applied pressure with her thumb and gently slid the lid out of its grooves. The silence of Edith's cottage absorbed her involuntary gasp. On a bed of green velvet lay a pair of dainty earrings. A lustrous round pearl was mounted to each gold screw, and from each setting hung a second pear-shaped pearl that swayed with any movement. The glowing sheen of the pearls reflected the flickering firelight. Responding to the inspiration of the moment, she reached up, and like a little girl playing dress-up, she screwed the earrings into place on her own ears. Nodding her head from side to side, she could feel the swaying pearls as they nuzzled her neck—like a mother's tender kisses. Time seemed to catch a breath. Rosamund slipped the lid back into place on the tiny box, but she left the earrings on her ears to continue their gentle ministration of whispered caresses. She placed the wooden box on the floor by the chest and reached up again to finger the pearl drops, to reaffirm this vicarious touch of her mother.

Suddenly eager to discover the chest's remaining treasures, she drew out a lumpy saffron-colored bag and quickly untied the drawstring cord. Although the silver was tarnished, the brushes contained in the bag were heavy, and the back of each one had been engraved with a scrolling *R*. Several glossy strands of long dark hair still clung to the stiff bristles, and Rosamund touched them in awe. They were a part of her mother—she had been a real person, not just the figment of a child's memory.

She picked up a brush, hesitated a moment, and then impetuously ran it through her own dark hair. In surprise, she heard herself humming a long-forgotten lullaby. She hummed it through a second time, brushing her hair with long, rhythmic strokes. The little lullaby and the gentle brushing seemed vaguely reminiscent of some sweet distant memory. When the melody ended, slowly, almost reluctantly, she arranged the brushes on the empty satin bag lying on the floor beside the wooden earring box. The firelight continued to illuminate the scrolling *R*s.

Rosamund's emotions were near the surface as she reached with anticipation into the chest for the third time and lifted out a baby's christening dress and matching bonnet. The delicate garments were yellowed with age and she wondered if the little frock and cap had been lovingly fashioned by her own young mother. She held up the bonnet and curled one hand into the crown. With the other hand she examined the even little stitches and gently smoothed the long silky ribbons. As she moved the bonnet this way and that with a turn of her wrist, a maternal longing poured over her like an ointment; she imagined that her hand was a baby's sweet head and she mused for a wistful moment on the mystery and joy of motherhood. Sighing deeply, she slipped the tiny cap from her curled fingers and tenderly laid it aside.

Holding up the dainty dress with its meticulous white-on-white embroidered bodice and rows of pleating along the lower section of the long skirt, she shook out time-pressed folds. As the wrinkles relaxed, so too did her self-control. Hugging the precious ceremonial dress close to her heart, she whispered brokenly, "Oh, Mama, I was your wee babe!"

Bittersweet. Joy and pain. Finding—and losing all over again. Brimming tears overflowed her eyes, and she sent them flashing away with a quick nod of her head. But more slipped in to take their place. Dropping her head, she sobbed her heartache into the sacred dress.

At last, caressing the gown and bonnet with loving fingers, as though reluctantly savoring the last of her mother's tenderness, Rosamund saw beyond herself sitting on the floor in front of an enameled box in the firelight of an old woman's cottage. The satin of the gown felt soft as a baby's skin; the armholes weren't much bigger around than her thumbs. And were those tiny faded spots trailing along the hem perhaps the wine of celebration? What a joyous occasion it must have been! How happy her young parents! So looking forward to the future. Little did they know what life held for them.

Her thoughts moved on. And now. What did life hold for her? Would love ever come to her? Would she one day be a mother? Someday know the miracle of new life? A shiver, almost a thrill of excitement, surged through her spirit. But the thrill was quickly followed by despair. She bit her lips to control the urge to cry again. Right now life held no promise of anything! With sharp, bitter movements she refolded the dainty garments and pushed away thoughts of her future.

Straightening her back, she deliberately reached again into the box. A final parcel wrapped in a silken scarf had been carefully fitted into the bottom of the chest. She lifted it out, wondering at its bulk. The fabric slipped off and landed in a swaddling drape across her lap. She couldn't help but exclaim when she saw that the object she held in her hands was a book. Indeed, a rare possession.

The gleaming cover of hand-tooled ivory was etched with delicately carved vines and flowers, and a small pearl formed the center of each flower—there were twenty-four in all. A large, oval ruby set in gold filigree, the cover's centerpiece, glistened in the firelight. Gold filigree corner protectors added to the beauty of the cover, and the wide, ornate clasp beckoned with the enigmatic charm of secret things waiting to be discovered. It was a Book of Hours, a nobleman's gift to his bride.

Her heart beating in her fingers, Rosamund carefully unfastened the clasp. With mounting excitement she raised the heavy cover. A pressed, dried yellow rose slid into her lap and nestled among the scarf's silken folds. She lifted the papery flower to smell its ageless fragrance, the scent of life and love, and then slipped it back in at the front of the book. The flower's significance—what had it been? She hoped the book would give her a clue to its meaning.

She held her breath in anticipation as she turned to the gold-edged presentation page. There, inscribed in her father's familiar flourishing hand, she read these startling words: *To my bride, the most fragrant Rose in the garden. With fondest affection. Nicklaus Schmidden.* The flower was surely a wedding rose! Her mother's wedding rose!

She wiped the sudden fresh flow of tears from her cheeks with her apron, a rough kiss of homespun. Her father's gentleness and quiet suffering flamed in her mind. She had always regarded the loss of her mother in terms of herself, but in this one moment the narrow boundaries of her self-focus broadened to include an awareness of the pain her father must have endured all these long years. His anguish had been far greater than her own. She didn't really know what she had missed.

But Papa! What agony! What torment! What despair! They had been there all along, carefully hidden. But she hadn't seen.

She drew in a ragged breath and continued her investigation of the book. Precise to the dotting of each *i* and the perfectly matched curls on the stems of every *y* and *g* and *j*, each handwritten page contained a passage from the book of Psalms, one psalm for each hour of a day. Colorful miniatures of plump cherubs, many-petaled delicate flowers, and trailing vines illuminated the pages. And each page was bordered by finely drawn tracery. The book was an exquisite work of art.

Following the pages of Scripture, a calendar listed the feast days of the church during a year. On the last page she found a prayer written by the scribe himself, and she lingered over the intimate words.

> Lord, send the blessing of Thy Holy Spirit
> upon this book, that it may mercifully enlighten
> our hearts and give us a true understanding, and
> grant that by its teaching it may brightly pre-
> serve and make full abundance of good works
> according to Thy will.

Rosamund closed her eyes in a surge of feeling, not just for the loss of her mother, nor for the beauty and heartbreak of her parents' love. She felt overwhelmed by the beauty of the prayer and the emptiness of her lonely heart; a heart longing for something that she couldn't identify.

Other than during that unusual conversation she'd had with her father several weeks ago, he had never men-

tioned God to her. Neither was God mentioned by the
servants or even her governesses—and Rosamund's
vague ideas of religion related to infrequent childhood
visits to the deserted Chapel of the Shepherd at Burg
Mosel. Once she had sat on a hard bench in the gloomy
sanctuary and wondered about the image of a Shepherd
cuddling a lamb that was illuminated in the stained
glass window. His kindly eyes touched her heart with an
oddly breathless feeling, and because there was no
explanation for the unusual sensation, she never went
back. Always, she told herself, it was just her imagination, not admitting to the secret longing of her soul.

She lowered the book to rest on her lap. Without
effort, it fell open near the center to Hour Twelve, and
she read the words:

> O God, thou art my God; early will I seek thee,
>   My soul thirsteth for thee,
> My flesh longeth for thee in a dry and thirsty land,
>   Where no water is. . .

"Yes, oh yes, that is me!" Rosamund exclaimed to
herself in a startled whisper.

> To see thy power and thy glory,
>   So as I have seen thee in the sanctuary.

Again she experienced the same breathless sensation
she had felt as a child when she had looked up with
wondering eyes at the Shepherd in the chapel window.
Hope stirred her soul—but it was followed by a cloud of
doubt. Could this feeling truly be God's presence, or

was she just generating an emotional experience out of her own desperate need? She read on:

> Because thy lovingkindness is better than life,
>> My lips shall praise thee.
> Thus will I bless thee while I live:
>> I will lift up my hands in thy name.
> My soul shall be satisfied as with marrow and fatness;
>> And my mouth shall praise thee with joyful lips:
> When I remember thee upon my bed,
>> And meditate on thee in the night watches.
> Because thou hast been my help,
>> Therefore in the shadow of thy wings will I rejoice.
> My soul followeth hard after thee:
>> Thy right hand upholdeth me.

The words jumped crookedly about the page until she blinked away the mist in her eyes.

> But those that seek my soul, to destroy it,
>> Shall go into the lower parts of the earth.
> They shall fall by the sword:
>> They shall be a portion for foxes.
> But the king shall rejoice in God;
>> Every one that sweareth by him shall glory:
> But the mouth of them that speak lies shall be stopped.
> —Psalm 63

The humble room faded into shadows without substance, and the unseen world became reality. What she had sensed *was* God's presence! He was *real,* and He had *spoken* to her! The light of wonder flooded in through the windows of her spirit. Warmth enveloped Rosamund, and she felt bathed in a wash of joy. Like a sponge, God's presence soaked up the pain and loneliness; she felt clean as a freshly scrubbed newborn. The balm of His comfort and peace soothed her aching soul. Swaddled in the softest white and cradled in gentle arms of love, Rosamund was held close to God's heart.

five

December had come and gone. It was January, and still there was no snow.

Every winter, navigation on the Baltic Sea was suspended. The northern regions of the sea would freeze, and although the southern waters remained navigable because of warm easterly winds and low salt content due to the many fresh water tributaries that emptied into it, frequent sudden storms blew through without warning. Choosing to be wise rather than sorry, seagoers spent winter on land, waiting for spring. This year, however, the warm easterly winds had been strangely silent, and unprecedented ice had formed over the entire sea.

The crisp frost that covered the ground crunched under Eric's feet as he determinedly made his way along the icy coast. His thoughts were on Lord Schmidden's request and his own inability to fulfill his obligation of honor. To come to the end of his personal resourcefulness had been the hardest thing he'd ever faced. Two things he dreaded: to quit and to fail. A very capable person, he was rarely at a loss for an answer, a decision, a solution. His unusual insight, even in his youth, had promoted him from crew member to captain, and his men risked their lives to his judgment.

Stomping forcefully toward his ship, he shook his head. Really, he would never have stayed in Sweden for the winter had he known the sea would freeze! Cold water was one thing; ice was quite another! The wooden planks of the ship would shrink, and her joints would pull apart. Months of repairs would be needed to make the vessel seaworthy again.

Looking up from the frosted strand where summer's grass resembled the underside of his mother's pincushion, Eric placed hand to brow against the winter sun. He studied his stately galleon with its brightly painted dragon's head carved into the anterior beam. Although he had chosen the vessel for its workmanship, the dragon's head, salvaged from the skeleton of a decaying Viking ship, had become the symbol of his invincibility.

Now his prowess was frozen solid. Cast in ice was his self-reliance. A sinking sense of frustration at his powerlessness overwhelmed him. He stepped out onto the frozen sea and moved close to the masthead. On impulse he reached out his hand to smooth it over the weathered carving. The enormity of its force was reduced to human terms.

He placed his hand against the prow, leaned his head on it, and closed his eyes. He stood there for long moments of tortured silence. His world had come to an icy end; his ship was more useless than the toy boats his father had carved for him when he was just a lad. Words of desperation were torn from his lips, "Oh God, help me understand."

When at last Eric straightened, he raised his head for a farewell look at that great symbol of his former strength. A strange thought brushed against the fringe of his mind. *Could it be that God is trying to redirect my life? He certainly has me immobilized. I wonder. . .*

Eric shrugged to dismiss the fleeting thought, and his gaze shifted downward from the dragon's head to his own feet that stood firm on the solid mass of ice. Suddenly, an unthinkable revelation exploded in his mind, a revelation as glorious as the Scandinavian summer's midnight sun. His body burned with daring and fear. His breath came in taut gasps, and every sea-hardened muscle tensed. Like breakers crashing against an impenetrable cliff, his sensibilities peaked and plummeted until his whole body dripped perspiration, spray in the wake of his revelation. The veil was rent. Sometimes fantasy is the beckoning light of faith. He *could* walk on water—*frozen* water!

𝕒

The downright absurdity of Eric's enterprise captivated the imagination of his crew. To a man, like exuberant schoolboys, they pooled their resources until every preparatory detail fell into place. Within a matter of days, twelve lightweight skiffs had been constructed and stood upright, leaning against the end wall of Olaf and Inga's cabin, awaiting departure.

Olaf and Inga had graciously made room for Eric to stay with them during this time of intense preparation and their home had become the headquarters for meetings and the storehouse for accumulating supplies. One end of the main room was piled high with folded teepee-like tents made of skins, and the supporting poles were propped outside next to the waiting skiffs. The crew had spent one whole day rehearsing "set up" and "take down" procedures to be sure each process could be accomplished quickly and smoothly.

Each man agreed to provide for himself warm furs:

outer hooded coat, leggings, mitts, and boots that could be lined with a thick layer of animal hair to insulate against the ice. Each would also provide two skin blankets for sleeping.

Soliciting dried fish and game from local villagers, friends, and relatives had evoked varied reactions to this unusual undertaking. People responded with everything from envy or encouragement to scorn and cynicism. But nothing dampened the men's enthusiasm.

In spite of criticism and ridicule, Eric proceeded with confidence. Never had he been so sure of himself. Yet his confidence was not in himself. He had discovered that at the end of self there is only God. And while the crew knew their leader intimately, suddenly it seemed like they didn't know him at all. He spoke and acted in an entirely new dimension of conviction quite different from his former boldness. His certainty hardened his crew's determination.

On the appointed departure date, dawn broke over the icy world and transformed every frost-covered tree and blade of grass into crystal. The sun's rays struck the ice, creating prisms of dancing color. It was as if God was smiling.

The crew of thirty-one men and the twelve skiffs bulging with supplies gathered at the wharf. Even though the penetrating cold leached life from everything it touched, local villagers (including the old men who wished they were young enough to join the expedition), a few friends, and family members came to wave them off. This would be a story to tell the grandchildren!

Eric reviewed basic instructions. "We will eat on the move. Do each of you have your provisions?" He waited for a nod from each of the men before continuing. "Daylight is so short at this time of year that we will not stop until dark. If you need to stop for any reason, it will be your responsibility to catch up. Stay alert! It is impossible to anticipate every potential danger. All right, any questions?" He looked around. "No? Then assume your positions."

The crew set off, resembling furry bears rather than toughened seamen. If all went as planned it would take two days to reach Europe's northern coast. Forty-five miles of ice!

One step at a time, they moved out onto the frozen sea. Like Moses and the children of Israel, for whom God parted the waters so they could cross on dry ground, Eric and his men witnessed God's power to command the elements of the natural world. He had spread out a pathway before their feet: water that was thick and sure.

Initially they set a rapid pace. The coastal ice was firm and solid, land was still in view, and the adrenaline of adventure bubbled in their veins. They laughed and joked as men do in the camaraderie of risking all.

The vast blue sky plunged down to outline the receding rugged coast, jagged peaks of far-off mountains, and a purple horizon that denied the reality of its distance. Patches of bare ice reflected the glimmering sun in a blinding glare that came and went without warning as they marched along.

Behind them the crusted land continued to shrink until finally, in every direction, thick-ribbed ice was all they could see. Late morning became midday, and the ebb and flow of conversation was like the tide, rising and falling. The air was clear and cold, and courage was at its peak.

When the sun eked its pale wintry light from its highest point on the horizon, what had appeared as a mirage in the distance became clearly visible. It was an island covered with trees. As they got closer, they could see animal tracks in the fine frost covering the ice. Rabbit. Bird. Deer. Footprints of the creatures who made the island their home.

And then, mingled with their marks of passing, Eric observed his own footprints, different in size and shape, yet nevertheless proclaiming that he, too, had been there and left an impact.

Early afternoon light faded into twilight and the men began to pace themselves, falling into cadence. Thud! Thud! Thud! Thud! Their footsteps pounded the ice. They were mesmerized, almost hypnotized by the monotony of their movements. Marching in rhythm was not a conscious decision. Rather, the behavior grew out of their ease with each other. Measured footsteps seemed to enhance that sense of security.

Suddenly everything changed. A loud bang, a thunderclap of earsplitting sound followed by another deafening crash, disrupted their complacency. Conversations broke in midsentence. In a split second, Eric assessed the situation. "Break cadence!" he shouted. "Move left!"

A near riot ensued as the men scrambled to safe ice. The rear guards who were closest to the growing hole could not find secure footing. They began to slip inexorably toward the black depths and certain death. Panting and heaving, the crew members closest to them pulled the rear guards to safety. While the crew watched from a safe distance, deadly black water swelled up to cover the place where they had once stood. The crew, to a man, was silent. The danger of their undertaking had struck hard.

The men regrouped, ready to move on as quickly as possible. Eric admonished the outer guards to be alert for more thin ice, and he instructed everyone to move at an individual pace. However, when the ice was solid from that point on, Eric concluded that they must have been near the center of the sea where ice formed last and was therefore the thinnest. If indeed that were true, then they had passed the halfway point.

The less time we spend on this ice, he said to himself, *the greater our chance of surviving this crossing without loss of life.*

As they continued to make progress, the texture of the ice began to change, and even though the men were weathered and hearty, the vigilance required to keep from tripping over wind ridges frozen in the ice, barely discernible in the fading daylight, caused them to quickly grow weary. Eric attempted to distract their minds from their herculean undertaking with a bit of humor.

"Suppose the earth really is flat after all. When it gets dark, who knows, we could fall off the edge!" His joke passed from man to man, and laughter dominoed from front guard to rear. It was only recently that the ancient idea of a flat earth had been disproved. The laughter diverted their minds from their tired backs and aching feet.

With refreshed spirits they picked up their lagging pace. Lively conversation ensued. Several debated whether or not the sea had ever before frozen solid. No one could recall any grandfather or older relative having mentioned such an unusual phenomenon.

Gradually conversation again gave way to concentration. Left foot. Right foot. Left foot. Right foot. One step at a time. Dusk settled rapidly, blue-gray and shadowy, and the stars appeared in the afternoon sky.

Olaf, covering the rear left corner, thought he heard something following him. Slowly he moved his head a quarter turn and shifted his gaze as far to the side as possible. There, stalking them but a short distance back, were eyes. Gleaming eyes! Malevolent eyes!

At first he couldn't quite make out the shapes, even though he could smell wild flesh. Suddenly one pair of eyes darted in closer. Despite the near darkness, he got a good look at a full-grown wolf. Its gray coat told him it was a European wolf, known for its innately aggressive behavior. And it was a thin wolf. A hungry wolf. The unusual weather had made prey difficult to find, and starving wolves make desperate predators.

Olaf hastily sent a message along the ranks, and at his signal the men halted their steps, turned, and raised their swords. Amid searing yelps, two wolves, lunging in midair, were cut down immediately. Warm blood squirted onto the ice and globbed into steamy hissing puddles beside the fallen carcasses.

Two wolves backed off into the shadows. Slowly they circled. Eyes gleaming. Fangs bared. Snarling. Voracious. A third sniffed frantically at the limp bodies of his fallen companions. They were still warm and bleeding. He raised his head and howled a mournful cry, eerie enough to send shivers splintering along Eric's veins. The crew drew back, bunching instinctively.

The lone wolf joined company once again with his

snarling fellows, and they moved in for a second attack. Hackles raised, ears swept back, and tails upright, two lean and desperate shadows darted straight in, heads down, taking dead aim for the men's vulnerable legs. The third gray form came in from the side with a powerful leap.

Instinctively, Olaf, object of the pouncing assault, stabbed his sword into the beast's silvery winter coat. Accompanied by wolf yelps and the mordant smell of dying flesh, Olaf shouted wildly and frantically thrust his sword again and again in desperate self-preservation. They fell together, man and wolf, with arms and legs flailing. Aghast, the men stood by. Helpless in their horror; they feared intervention would cause more harm than good.

The remaining two wolves, diverted by the fall of Olaf and their companion predator, crouched to pounce on the tangled pair; whether to assist in the attack or to take advantage of their partner's kill could hardly be determined in the panic of the moment. However, quick thinking on the part of Reed and Dugan put an end to the momentary threat of such a tragedy. Lunging at the wolves from either side, they brought their swords crashing down on the backs of the two beasts. Those standing closest heard the bones snap as both rapacious wolves slammed onto the bloody arena.

Olaf rolled away from the still twitching carcass of the wolf he had just killed, and although he was not seriously injured, when he tried to stand his legs gave out and he began to shake violently. Fellow crew members, snapping out of their paralyzing stupor of horror, gathered around him. Karl responded to Eric's order to bring a blanket, and the two of them wrapped Olaf tightly in the thick skin and strapped him securely on the nearest skiff.

One. Two. Three. Four. Five. The wolves lay dead on the ice. They left them where they had fallen; grisly shadows of death.

Progress resumed—and so did discussion! Each crew member had his own impressions of what had just happened, and after the attack had been discussed from every angle, the talk branched off into other tales of prowess and daring adventure.

Bone-weary and longing for sleep, the men lapsed into silent. Even Olaf, who had mercifully fallen asleep on the skiff, stopped snoring. They were alone, isolated by the darkness. Each crew member concentrated on placing one foot in front of the other, and discouragement goaded them toward despair. Morning would never come. Land was nowhere to be found.

They had been foolhardy to even make such an attempt. Olaf—not to mention the rest of them—had come very close to being ripped to pieces by wild beasts! They should never have listened to Eric. What had happened to their common sense? How could they have been so foolish?

Eric, while aware of his men's discouragement, had determined to keep going until a significant distance separated them from the dead wolves. His best judgment told him distance would provide a measure of safety.

But finally, after what seemed like an endless trek under the night sky, Eric called for a halt. The men responded with relief and rapidly set up camp. Dull orange light produced by several whale oil lanterns cast eerie mocking shadows that lurked and pounced as the tent poles were fanned out on the frozen sea like the spokes of a wheel. The tent skins were placed over the poles, and then, with one man lifting each pole, the tents were raised to an upright position. The top ends of the poles extended out through the small circular opening at the center of each skin, and the bottom ends were lowered into holes etched in the ice. The upright tents stood around the skiffs like sentries standing guard.

Next came tent assignments, and Eric reminded the men to sleep on top of their skin blankets and to remain clothed for maximum warmth. One crew member from each tent was assigned to take first turn at watch duty. Within minutes, the entire crew had retired for the night.

Eric moved quickly from tent to tent, checking on the men and speaking briefly with those on watch. When he felt certain everything was secure, he slipped into his own assigned tent space and unrolled his skin blankets. Stretching out on his back, he crossed his arms behind his head and looked up into the darkness. A few shining stars winked at him through the small hole at the top of the tent. He always loved to watch them, to think of their vastness, their distance, and of their well-ordered march across the sky. In that instant he felt God's eye upon him, a protecting Presence. A trusting smile turned up the corners of Eric's mouth, and he closed his eyes.

Shortly before daybreak, the men on final watch woke the crew, and everyone quickly rose and bound up their skins. While some men dismantled the tents, others reloaded the skiffs. A third group made a fire with kindling they had brought along. They placed a block of ice in a metal cauldron suspended over the fire to provide drinking water. When each one had satisfied his thirst and every item had been carefully returned to its place, the crew set out on the second day of their incredible adventure.

But somehow the novelty had worn thin; the men lacked enthusiasm, and time seemed to drag. A chill wind came up and scuttled dark clouds across the sky until they blotted out the thin light from the winter sun. Dry crystals of loose ice blew up to sting their faces, and a dense fog settled down around them, reducing visibility and hampering progress. The combination of cold wind and damp fog stiffened their furs until walking became a chore. Their labored breathing sounded like bellows wheezing over a reluctant fire, and vapor turned to ice and clung to their lashes and beards. They trudged along for hours, miserable and weary. No one conversed; each man carefully expended only the barest minimum of energy.

In the late afternoon, exhausted and nearly frozen on his feet, Dugan, one of the front guards, stumbled over something frozen in the ice. Slowly, stiffly, he bent over, determined to investigate. A stiff tuft of grass sticking up through the ice had tripped him. Elated, he bellowed out a lusty roar, "Land!" Although the fog was so thick that they could not see more than a few feet ahead, the men forgot their tiredness and set off running the final distance, hooting and yelling, And when their feet crunched on icy soil, the whoops of elation were so loud they could have cracked the ice—but no one cared. Land at last!

Eric closed his eyes and released the air from his lungs. So great was the relief that he felt light-headed. Never had he doubted the outcome of this endeavor, but the wonder of living minute by minute through a miracle, of being suspended in God's revealed hand, was unlike anything he had ever experienced. It reminded him of coming in from the cold. Nose, ears, fingers, and toes sting and tingle. And then the whole body flushes with heat until every nerve comes shouting into life. His whole being stung and tingled with revelation and then flushed in acute awareness of God's presence. He raised his hands to God in awe at the incredible demonstration of God's power he had just witnessed.

The men, too, were nearly hysterical. They boosted Eric to their shoulders and cavorted about in frenzied excitement. Disillusionment and despair were quite forgotten. They had accomplished the impossible!

When camp had again been established, the men fell into welcome sleep. But Eric, restless from the excitement and noting that a wind had come up and blown away the fog, set off by himself to walk and think. Solitude and contemplation had been vital elements of his past successes, and he could not ignore them during his present challenge. Tomorrow would see his men begin the final leg of their trek, the overland march to Burg Mosel, and he knew he would again have to consider the welfare of the group above his own needs.

But tonight he needed time alone.

six

Rosamund, alone in Edith Baer's cottage, had all but forgotten that time in the physical realm keeps a dutiful pace. An hour passed in what seemed like a moment.

Then, intruding on her solitude, there came a firm knock on the crude wooden door. Rosamund jumped up to open it, her face shining with God's love. She tugged at the heavy bar and pushed open the door, a joyous welcome for Edith on her lips. But glad words froze in her throat as she gasped at the overwhelming fur-cloaked figure that loomed in front of her. Instead of Edith's wizened, smile-creased face, a pair of eyes the blue of Nordic sky greeted her from between frosty golden lashes.

Shocked, Rosamund stood paralyzed. Color came and went in her face. She opened her mouth but still no words came. She knew those eyes! In a flash she was nine years old again—and he was her childhood hero!

"Good evening. My name is Eric Branden. I walked around the point and intended to go straight back, but I came farther than I'd planned." He spoke with ease and confidence, as one who lives with purpose. "Could I rest by your fire?"

The deep voice with its rich accent jerked Rosamund abruptly back to the present. In her struggle to maintain a semblance of dignity, she backed out of the doorway and stammered in jerky sentences, "Please come in. Forgive my rudeness. I was expecting someone else. I'll lay more wood on the fire. You can put your things here on the bench. Would you like a hot drink?"

She fluttered about nervously while the tall, broad-shouldered young man emerged from his fur cocoon. At nine years old, she had idolized him. He had treated her with dignity and respect, unlike most of her father's friends who ignored her, teased her, or found children a nuisance. But now she was an adult, and it occurred to her that he probably wasn't really as wonderful as she remembered, even though rich memories flooded her mind: memories of riding the horses along the beach at Feste Burg. Wading barefoot in the shallow water. Laughing when waves pounding against the nearby cliffs covered them with friendly spray. Collecting shells. Learning about the little creatures that had once made those shells their homes. Studying the stars at night. Discovering she could identify the Hunter and the Crab, the Dippers, and the North Star.

She knew she had asked a thousand questions. Too many questions. But he had always been patient. And somehow he knew all the answers. He had taken her aboard his ship and let her watch from a safe distance while he and his men made repairs on a damaged sail rigging. He had shown her the fascinating charts by which he navigated. A good teacher to an eager and adoring pupil.

Eric had been her first exposure to a male companion outside of her father. But the days of his stay had passed all too quickly. The repairs had been completed, and Eric and his crew had set sail once again. And no one knew that every spring saw her anxious to make the move to their summer residence at Feste Burg. Always, there was the secret hope that Eric would come back. She climbed the stairs to the top of the tower every morning to look out to sea, checking the horizon for a certain ship. But it never came again.

At last she had put the memory away with other childhood treasures. And now, here he was, in Edith's cottage!

She eyed him critically. He still had the same strong jaw and boyish smile—just as she remembered. Handsome, yes. But more than that. He had developed deeper strength, maturity, an intangible suggestion of spiritual stature. Or could it be that she had matured?

Eric, unaware of her scrutiny, looked around the humble cottage. His gaze touched on the open chest with its contents heaped on the floor in front of it, and he was suddenly aware he had interrupted this peasant girl's evening. He apologized, "Please forgive me for disturbing you."

"It's all right," she said, quick to reassure him. "I've been going through a box of keepsakes." With a graceful gesture she indicated the collection of treasures he had noticed. Not sure she knew how to explain the significance of her evening, she drew her dark brows together before continuing, "Tonight I found some things that had belonged to my mother. . ." Delight at being once again with this dear friend made her add impulsively, "And tonight I found God!"

Rosamund bent to pick up the Book of Hours that had slid from her lap to the floor when she had jumped up to answer the knock at the door. "Look!" Eagerly, she handed the volume to Eric and pushed his furs to one end of the bench so they could sit down. Completely unself-conscious in her desire to share her joy, Rosamund hovered near his elbow; in her excitement she did not realize that Eric had not recognized her.

Puzzled by the girl's open friendliness, Eric stole several glances at her. The firelight had turned Rosamund's roughly woven dress to velvet; her eyes glistened, and soft curls framed her sweet upturned face. Her beauty was not lost on him, but it was overshadowed by a nagging sense of familiarity. Unable to identify who she reminded him of, he shrugged to himself and turned his attention to her book.

Books were rare, and this one was obviously a very special one. He held it firmly on his knees and carefully opened the clasp with hard, muscular hands. When he lifted the cover, the heavy binding creaked. He turned the first few blank pages, and when he reached the presentation page, the pressed yellow rose slid out. Rosamund quickly retrieved it, cradling it in her lap.

Eric's eyes fell to the inscription. His face registered visible shock. "Nicklaus Schmidden!" The exclamation burst from him. One thought chased another, and he looked at her again, intently. "Why, you're little Rosamund!" Astonishment filled his voice. "Rosamund Schmidden!" No wonder she seemed so familiar! "But what are you doing here?" his voice sharpened. "Why aren't you with your father?"

Little Rosamund! His words smarted like sand flung in her face. He still thought of her as a child. *And after all, what was* he *doing here?* she thought warily. With her father's parting words of caution still echoing loudly in her ears, she answered coldly, "I live here." The finality of her reply discouraged further questioning, and Eric, sensing her withdrawal, looked down at the book he still held. His mind spun like a wooden top, trying to balance the past with the present. What had he said to put her off? There were at least a dozen questions he would like to ask—questions about her father, about the threatened attack, about the summons for help, about why she was living here, about the years that had passed since last they met—but she had made it obvious she didn't want him to ask.

Diplomatically, he changed the direction of the conversation. "You said you found God?" he questioned. This could prove a touchy subject as well, but she had brought it up—and it was worth the risk. He looked down at the book to give her space.

To his surprise and satisfaction, she answered immediately. "Oh, yes!" All the joy and healing she had experienced in the preceding hour found expression in those two words, and his eyes instinctively sought hers. Rosamund returned his look without faltering, although it seemed to her his piercing gaze probed into her mind, indeed plunged to her very soul. At length he nodded, as though satisfied, "I, too, have found God!"

The world of Edith's primitive cottage slipped into the shadows. Eric was forgiven for referring to Rosamund as a child, and her soul answered his in wordless conversation as they both realized that they belonged to God in the same special way.

But for Eric it was more than that. It was as if a curtain had been torn away. This lovely girl was the child he had known! Her boyishness had disappeared, and she was a woman now—a beautiful woman. Her long dark lashes shadowed the deep blue of her eyes. He saw the beauty of her half-parted lips, the throbbing hollow at her throat, the soft roundness of her maidenly figure. That heady scent, desire, permeated his senses. To kiss her! To hold her! He smiled grimly to himself. And to think he'd wondered as the years passed if he was capable of such feelings!

His fingers tightened on the Book of Hours until his knuckles showed white and the blood pounded in his temples. What to do with this kindredness of spirit that expressed itself in a desire to know her on every level? To know her in the warm shadows of this world and in the blinding glory of spiritual oneness. To merge the two realms into one. He was just being foolish, he admonished himself sternly. His nerves were overwrought from the past month of preparations and the last few days of excitement. She probably hardly remembered him, he reasoned; she had been so young. With great effort he refocused his attention on her earlier comment, forcing out a question in what he hoped would pass for a normal voice, "And your mother?"

"Papa never told you about her?" She questioned him in surprise.

Eric shook his head. Still grappling with his reeling senses, words would not come.

"I don't remember much about her. She was lost when I was only five. . ." A surge of emotion choked off her voice.

"Lost. . ." Eric echoed the word as if he had not heard right. He was disturbed by the sudden distress on her face. The urge to comfort her thundered in his chest. But years of mastery over himself stood him in good stead, and he remained motionless.

She confided apologetically, "It sounds unbelievable, I know. I suppose that's why we never talk about it." She clasped her hands together so tightly that her nails dug into her soft skin. "I can only tell you what I remember. My mother's cousin, Lady Josie, was getting married, and there was a lot of excitement at Burg Mosel."

Once she started to talk, the long pent-up words and emotions poured out in a torrent. She stared into the fire. "I had a new blue frock. And my first pair of dress-up gloves; they were made of white leather and they had tiny rosebuds embroidered on them."

She tipped her head slightly, as if seeing the events all over again, and her long curling hair that brushed against his shoulder sent a shock through Eric's whole body.

"Mother was so beautiful," Rosamund continued, oblivious to Eric's heightened senses. "She wore a tiara in her hair. Papa called her his queen. . .and I was his fairy princess." She smiled at the memory. "I vaguely remember the beautiful music and the strange, sweet smell of incense. Candlelight flickered on the saints painted on the walls and made them seem alive. And Lady Josie looked so happy. After the wedding there was a party. Nurse gave me a piece of fruitcake and some hot cider. The cake was so delicious that I sneaked a second piece. Nurse came just then to take me away to get ready for bed. I didn't want her to know I had taken more cake so I hid my hand behind my back. The cake stained my new frock and she scolded me for being greedy. She said God would punish me. I felt so ashamed that I cried myself to sleep." Rosamund pressed her fingers to her lips, as if the memory was still painful.

"Later I was told the guests had played games after I went to bed. During hide-and-seek, my mother went to hide. Several guests saw her go down the hall toward the chapel." She stopped.

"Yes?" Eric prompted softly.

"That was the last anyone ever saw her. Everyone searched, but nobody found her—and she never came back. Ever."

Tears glistened on her lashes as she went on to confide her inmost childhood fear. "I thought it was my fault—that God was punishing me." She hesitated, considering, and then confided, "Papa blamed God. He's ignored God ever since." The suspended tears spilled down her cheeks, and she quickly reached up to whisk them away.

"F-forgive me for being so emotional," she whispered, "but you asked."

Eric swallowed the lump in his throat. He had remained still while Rosamund spoke, fearing to disrupt the trusting exposure of feelings hidden deep in her heart. Hope arose within him that in her own way she might be revealing the same desire to know and be known by him as he felt toward her. Abandoning caution, he reached out his hand to comfort her.

At that critical moment, urgent pounding shook the door. Rosamund's attention was instantly diverted. She jumped up to answer the knock, leaving Eric's consoling touch suspended in midair.

Wiping her eyes on the corner of her apron, she cleared her throat and raised the bar before pushing the door open. A burly, bearded fellow filled the doorway and then stepped boldly inside. He pulled the door shut behind himself and demanded the crock of dried mustard stored on a ledge of the fireplace. "Edith needs it," he said gruffly.

"Emil, this is Eric Branden, an old friend of mine." With that brief introduction, Rosamund turned toward the fireplace, and the two men watched her as she reached up to get the jar of mustard. Her curling hair and slender, womanly figure embraced by the warmth of the humble cottage fireplace flamed a poignant tableau of domesticity that caused Eric to flinch. The long-suppressed yearning for a place of his own, shared with someone special to make it a home, surged like a flood within Eric's thoughts.

Rosamund turned toward Emil Lanz, Edith Baer's closest neighbor, with a warm, open smile. Jealousy stabbed Eric with its dagger. Did Rosamund's smile contain something more than friendship? Who was this fellow, anyway? He was obviously very at home in this cottage and comfortable with Rosamund. Did she belong to him? Was he good enough for her? Eric bit down hard on the inside of his cheek, and the warm taste of blood mingled with the juices in his mouth.

The brusque visitor shot a piercing look at Eric, nodded his head in curt acknowledgment, and left Edith's cottage just as abruptly as he'd come. He slammed the heavy door with what to Eric seemed an unnecessarily loud bang, but it served to remind him that he had quite forgotten time and responsibility. He jumped up, exclaiming, "I must be going!" He avoided Rosamund's eyes. Unfamiliar feelings still threatened to suffocate him, and he knew a desperate urgency to get away at once.

While Eric swiftly encased himself in his heavy furs,

Rosamund stood watching him in silent dismay. He had just come. And now he was leaving. She lifted her chin, and their eyes met. The burning light in his startled her. What did it mean? She was sure it hadn't been there earlier.

Eric froze, speechless as a school boy. He knew he had to go. But he wanted to stay.

Under his speaking gaze, a slow flush caressed her cheeks, her chest rose and fell with a soft, quick gasp, and her dark lashes dropped to hide her confusion. In the awkward intensity of the moment she nervously spoke the first thing that came to her mind. "It's snowing! I hope you don't have far to go?"

How foolish! she thought. But, in fact, her mundane words bridged the uncomfortable gap between heart-to-heart contact and the reality of his leave-taking. They both tried to pretend nothing had happened between them.

Eric reached out and clasped her slender hand in his mitted grasp. "Good-bye, Rosamund. God keep you. . ." Unsaid words hung in the space between them as he hesitated. He gave her hand a quick squeeze and then, with a searching look that said too much—yet not quite enough—he was gone.

Dazed, Rosamund stood in the doorway, her slender shape outlined by the firelight streaming from behind her. Eric took several steps, turned to look back, and raised a mitted hand in farewell. Resuming his pace, head down, he faded into the kaleidoscope of softly falling snow, alone in the darkness with his soul-shaking discovery.

Rosamund shut out the pinching cold and sank down on the floor beside the vacant bench, like a rag doll without its stuffing. "Eric Branden. How amazing!" she whispered under her breath. She hadn't thought of him in a long time. The look in his eyes! She flushed again, even though there was no one to see. She knew Eric no longer regarded her as a child.

Several hours later Edith pounded and pounded on the heavy wooden door. Rosamund finally roused. She had fallen asleep on the floor, leaning against the bench in front of the dying fire. With her head cradled in her arm she had dreamed of walking in the castle garden at Burg Mosel and filling a flower basket with roses. Yellow roses.

ⁱᵃ

Snow stung his cheeks and clung to his eyelashes as Eric Branden determinedly retraced his steps. The night sky was gray, and the rocks along the coast were gray, too. The earth and sky seemed to run together. It was hard to tell where one stopped and the other started when everything was shrouded in a misty veil of lightly falling snow.

Eric didn't notice. Memories dominated his thoughts. In his mind he pictured the precocious daughter of Lord Schmidden as she had been seven years before: thin and gangly, with bright eyes that were too large for her small face. She had reminded him of his younger sister, Karena, who was about Rosamund's age, and her eager questions had made him feel knowledgeable and important. He had enjoyed telling her exciting tales from his seafaring adventures. She had listened in rapt wonder, often exclaiming, "Did you really?" and "You're so brave!" just like Karena.

But little Rosamund had grown up. He had seen one

friend after another grow soft toward a girl, but he saw now that their actions had been but the smoke of a volcano. Fire and darkness, ecstasy and terror, all rushed over him, and he was glad for the cold and the snow. The more he thought about the last hour, the faster he walked. And the faster he walked, the more questions shot through his mind. Why was she living here? Who was the fellow who had come demanding mustard? He had certainly been bold, quite as if he owned the place! And, Eric recalled, Rosamund did say she was expecting someone else. Fear cast a long shadow. Was that churlish man her husband? He winced as though he had been stabbed. Oh, surely not! She seemed so innocent. And yet. . . Over and over his mind replayed the events of the evening. Over and over he asked the same torturing questions. Questions without answers.

As he neared the hastily assembled camp, his steps grew slower. Odd how his heart just hours before had pumped with the thrill of *fait accompli*. Amazing how a girl's sweet face could completely eclipse even the surge of triumph at a legend-building sea crossing.

seven

Dark and brooding against the deep blue of a late January afternoon sky, Burg Mosel loomed above the white mist lying low in the surrounding valleys. Wood smoke scented the air, and a crimson winter sun spotlighted the turrets of the stone residence that towered above it. The castle appeared to float, suspended on a magic carpet of clouds.

Inside the guest room on the second floor of the main tower, Eric Branden stood staring at the orange and scarlet flames leaping in the fireplace. The blaze threw lively patterns on the bare wood-paneled walls and sent gloomy shadows skulking away to hide behind the bed curtains.

While he waited for a servant to take him to meet Lord Schmidden, Eric surveyed his assigned domain. Along one wall there were shelves for his belongings. A small bedside table held a bowl and pitcher, and a towel for a quick wash hung from a nearby peg. A skin rug sprawled between two large wooden chairs, one with a foot bench situated conveniently before it. These were the only furnishings besides a large tub for bathing, the curtained bed, and the candle stands which burned brightly with multiple candles. It was definitely a man's room: utilitarian in every way.

When Eric and his crew had arrived at Burg Mosel in

the early afternoon following a two-day march inland from the sea, capable servants had quickly established the men in simple guest quarters that opened off the corridors on both levels of the rear wing of the castle. When their care was assured, Eric followed a servant through the main entrance, down the corridor that passed the chapel, and up a broad curving stone stairway to this spacious room high up in the tallest tower. A commanding view of the valleys and villages below would be his on a clear day, but the heavy mist suited his mood exactly. He felt melancholy, almost morose.

The miracles of a willing crew and a frozen sea had buoyed him with faith and anticipation. Now, however, his pulsating thoughts continually reverted to a humble cottage on the coast, and each time he closed his eyes he saw Rosamund's feminine shape outlined in the open doorway. She was indelibly impressed upon his mind. Shining waves of dark hair. Rosy, dimpled cheeks. Smiling lips. And clear, blue eyes.

If it wasn't enough to think about her all the time, nagged by the thought that she belonged to another, now he must stay in her home, visit with her father. Uncertainty stung him like salt water in a rope burn. Then, at the sound of approaching footsteps, he lifted his head, straightened his shoulders, and determined to accept reality, whatever he might discover it to be, as God's plan for him.

In response to the summoning knock, Eric followed the servant out into the stone stairwell and down the steps that wound to the left, a design giving the defender in a sword fight an advantage because he would always be turning his sword arm toward his enemy. At the bottom of the steps, Eric followed along the wide-windowed corridor which at night would be shuttered closed and lit by the candles set in shoulder-high sconces. They passed heavy double doors on the left that were chained shut, and Eric turned his head for a second look before hurrying to keep up with his guide. The corridor extended into the elaborate entrance hall where dark eyes in stiff canvas faces stared down at him.

Eric followed the servant across the entrance hall and along the continuing corridor that stretched the length of the right wing and opened into the dining room and the great room. Hearing their footsteps on the resounding marble, Lord Schmidden rose to his feet in anticipation.

The two men greeted each other warmly.

"The sight of you is a relief to my eyes, Branden!" Lord Schmidden declared. He appeared steady and controlled, but inward excitement surged recklessly. The plan just might work! Each step had happened so smoothly that his faith was rapidly being restored.

He drew a second chair near his own that faced the roaring fire and motioned to Eric to be seated. Pausing briefly at the sideboard, he selected two heavy goblets and generously filled them from one of the many available decanters. He handed one to Eric, and he took the second with him to his waiting chair.

Eric glanced quickly around, observing the formality of the room: richly embroidered draperies, delicate chairs, brocade-covered settees, marble-topped tables displaying *objets d'art*. The exceptions were these two chairs which had obviously been chosen for comfort, and a low wooden stool to the left of the hearth that sat askew as if it had been impatiently scooted out of the way.

The fireplace was oversized, befitting the vastness of the room; a tall man could stand inside at the peak of the arch, and Eric guessed it was probably wide enough for five or six large men to stand side by side within its mouth. Mounted above it, a life-size canvas drew his eyes like a magnet. He caught a sharp breath; for a fleeting moment he thought Rosamund had come to haunt him. On second look, he realized it must be her mother—but the resemblance certainly intrigued him, and he forced himself to look away for fear he would embarrass himself by staring.

Lord Schmidden noted his guest glancing around the room and he waved a deprecating hand toward the ornate furnishings, "It's the fireplace I come here for— it's the best one in the place."

Eric nodded.

Conversation flowed easily as the two men emptied their glasses and reviewed the past seven years, including Lord Schmidden's urgent request for assistance, Eric's ensuing despair, and the divine revelation that led to his miraculous crossing. Lord Schmidden did not comment on Eric's references to God's intervention— habitual self-reliance is not easily admitted to nor relinquished. By nature a cautious man, Lord Schmidden needed time to think about what he had just heard.

Presently, Eric questioned Lord Schmidden, "What is your current situation, sir? How may I help you?"

Lord Schmidden, in a few short sentences, outlined the villagers' squabbling and raiding, and mentioned his own efforts to restore peace. "I thought things had settled down, but when we returned to Burg Mosel at the end of summer, Lord Frederick came to see me. We sat talking, right here, just like you and I are doing. I expected we'd finalize the details of our agreement. Instead, he questioned me about Rosamund—you remember my daughter?"

Eric nodded. His heart began to pound, his mouth went dry, and his hands clenched into fists involuntarily. He could feel the heat rising up his neck to stain his face.

Intent on the fire, bushy brows drawn down to meet each other, Lord Schmidden remained unaware of Eric's revealing countenance. He continued, "He asked her age, and if she was married. And did I have other children?" I reluctantly answered his questions, and then he informed me he'd met Rosamund earlier in the spring when she'd been out walking. He said he liked her spirit and he wanted to marry her."

Eric broke out in a cold sweat and braced himself. He had already determined not to ask questions or push himself on Lord Schmidden. When he knew if Rosamund was free, then and only then would he be in a position to ask for Rosamund's hand in marriage. And if indeed she was free, her father might not be willing to give her to him—or she might not be interested in marrying him. But surely her eyes had given him hope!

Lord Schmidden leaned forward as he confided, "I may not be a seer, but I know Lord Frederick doesn't care a boar's head about my Rosamund. He's ambitious—and not even subtle about it! Rosamund is young and beautiful now, but how could I be sure that once my property was safely in his pocket he'd still be kind to her, especially as she ages. Or to me, for that matter! I'd just be a stone under a pestle." He gestured forcefully with his empty goblet.

"So what did you tell him?" Eric unconsciously held his breath.

"I told him no, of course!"

"And thus his threat of an all-out war?"

"Precisely."

"And. . .your daughter?" He found he couldn't say her name. "How did she feel about all this?" He must know the whole truth.

Lord Schmidden rose deliberately and moved again to the sideboard. He poured Eric another drink and refilled his own before he slowly turned to answer. "I didn't tell her about Lord Frederick's visit or demands, and I didn't tell her about sending to you for help. I sent her to stay with Edith, my childhood nurse—so even if I'm defeated, at least she'll be safe." He emptied his goblet in a single gulp. "And now that you're here, well, I'm confident that won't happen." He banged the goblet down on the wood surface with an emphatic thud.

Eric affirmed, "With God's help, I won't fail." It was a vow.

Strange how the room suddenly felt so very warm! Eric scooted his chair away from the fire. He stretched out his legs and leaned his head against the back of his chair. As he closed his eyes, he felt the tension leave his body. Relief melted him to his seat. Rosamund was free! Unseemly shadows of the danger of being attracted to another man's wife evaporated, and his heart floated up to dance with the frescoed ceiling cherubs.

Lord Schmidden returned to his chair, and they sat on in companionable silence.

When the fire began to die down, Lord Schmidden

rose to rebuild it. He stacked the fireplace with huge logs that snapped and crackled and radiated warmth. Still standing in front of the rekindled flames, Lord Schmidden began to talk as though now that the immediate challenge of Lord Frederick's threatened attack had a foreseeable solution, he could share his inmost thoughts.

"Aggressors continue their push to conquer the world. Just look at France and England! Why, they've been at each other for over fifty years! I've been wondering if Lord Frederick isn't a functionary, sent to establish a foothold here. Obviously the strategy is different, at least initially, but forcing me to allow him to marry my daughter so he can gain control of the largest section of land in this region would certainly give him a base for conquering the rest."

He turned to poke aggressively at the blazing logs with a heavy fire iron. "That's another reason why I was afraid of this proposed marriage. We could lose much more, even, than each other." He leaned the fire iron against the stones and dropped heavily into his chair. "I suspect he's come with backing from somewhere. It's a costly business to build a fortress these days. And his administrator! He's an acorn in a willow tree! He's not from around here, of that I'm certain!"

He shifted in his chair and brought a heavy boot up to rest on the knee of the other leg. "I've traveled the trade routes, you know. Years ago the Romans came, bringing their religion and government with them, and they confiscated the possessions of anyone who didn't conform and support their system. He shrugged, "It's just a feeling, if you will, but I can't seem to shake it."

Physically as restless as his thoughts, he stood again and moved over to the fireplace, where he stabbed distractedly at the flaming logs. Still grasping the awkward iron, he swung about abruptly, "This is *my* property." He pounded the iron on the hearthstone for emphasis and continued in an uncharacteristically strident voice. "Has been for generations, and I wouldn't take kindly to giving service to another!"

Eric sat silent, considering the older man's opinions. When he finally spoke it was with caution. "Your concerns may very well be valid. Only the future—"

Loud voices echoed in the entrance hall. Their conversation broke off as they strained to hear the cause of the commotion. A flustered maid appeared in the doorway. Following a quick curtsy, she announced that a messenger from Lord Frederick was waiting to see Lord Schmidden.

"Show him in," Lord Schmidden directed. With eyebrows raised, he and Eric exchanged a knowing glance and stood to their feet.

In a moment Matilda reappeared, followed by a short, squatty man. His pompous manner and gaudy apparel evoked immediate distrust in Eric. He recalled his mother's oft-repeated advice, "Folks lacking substance on the inside draw attention to themselves with exaggerated dress or manner."

Without even waiting for Lord Schmidden to address him, the obnoxious fellow began to speak. His heavy accent and sentence structure indicated a foreign heritage. "Louie, I am, overseer for the Lord Frederick." He pulled on his piebald goatee with fleshy hands—first one and then the other. Several gold rings on his stubby fingers flashed in the firelight, and his beady black eyes glittered with condescension.

"A message from Lord Frederick I bring you. He awaits your reconsideration of the matter of his marriage to your daughter. Time enough he has given you." He pursed his thin lips. "He expects you to send word to him through me of the date you choose for the marriage. He wishes to offer to the Lady Rosamund his deepest respect and a visit to arrange at once." He smiled importantly, as though he expected to be treated with deference.

Where Rosamund was concerned, Lord Schmidden's emotions betrayed his ability to treat a situation objectively. Even as Louie spoke, Lord Schmidden's face grew red and a muscle twitched in his left cheek. One hand clenched the tall wooden chairback beside him, and Eric heard a low growl beginning to rumble in his throat.

Sensing Lord Schmidden's emotional reaction outstriding any shrewdly calculated response, Eric quickly broke in to preserve the fragile peace. His voice was smooth yet carried the sense of one who expects to be obeyed without question. "Thank you for your visit today, Louie. Lord Schmidden has no message for Lord Frederick at this time. When he does, he will contact Lord Frederick. Can I help you find your way out?"

Eric took several steps toward the little man, who drew himself up like a Bantam rooster and went strutting toward the door. What he lacked in height he made up for in manner. Eric followed him down the hallway to insure his leave-taking. He half-expected the offensive fellow would consider inordinate persistence to be a virtue.

Lord Schmidden, waiting in the great room, regained

his equanimity, and when Eric returned he expressed his astonishment, "Why didn't you tell that rooster that I'd never, under any circumstances, give my Rosamund to Lord Frederick?!"

"Well, sir," Eric replied contemplatively, "I'd say that discretion is the key to winning a war. A message sent by the enemy's ambassador won't be the same by the time it's delivered. Oh, the words may be the same—but that's not all there is to communication. . ." His words trailed off. He hadn't meant to sound so condescending.

But Lord Schmidden nodded, his confidence in Eric's judgment rising to a new height. "Ah, yes, I can see your point. So what do you suggest we do now?"

The two men began discussing strategy in earnest.

eight

The pungent aroma of herbs laced the air in Edith's cottage. A February blizzard had been tormenting the sky for three long days and no one, not even the determined Edith, ventured out. A smothering net of white haze clouded the atmosphere. Angry winds screamed at each other, causing Edith's house to creak and shudder. Rosamund, unaccustomed to such close proximity to the elements, not to mention Edith's hearty snoring, managed only fitful spurts of sleep.

Each morning Edith had cautiously eased open the heavy door to survey the outside world, and each time, the ripping wind nearly tore it from her hands. Resigned to confinement, they had carefully rationed Edith's meager stack of wood. By sliding the rough bench close to the fireplace and steadying it with bits of loose bark wedged under the high end, they were able to take full advantage of the fire's warmth and live in relative comfort.

Never idle, Edith had pulled stalks of dried herbs down from the rafters. In summer she had gathered, bundled, and hung them upside down to dry. Because various herbs must be collected at differing stages in their development, Edith often said with a chuckle that continually looking forward to gathering the next herb crop was what kept her young! Everyone laughed along with her, for she was by far the oldest villager—having seen eighty-four birthdays come and go.

Rosamund held a kettle in her lap, and one at a time, snapped free the brittle herb leaves from their stems. The discarded stalks crackled merrily in the fire, and the mound of leaves in her kettle steadily grew under her nimble fingers. Two weeks had passed since "The Night of the Book," as Rosamund called it in her thoughts. She had not spoken of it, nor of Eric's visit. Sometimes disclosing special events to someone else lessens their value, so she had hesitated, wanting to talk yet reluctant to spoil the wonder of her experience.

Covertly, Edith observed her young guest, whose bright eyes brimmed with her unvoiced thoughts. Once Rosamund even opened her mouth as though to speak, and then, hesitating a second, pressed her lips firmly closed. Several times her hands fell idle as she stared into the fire. With wisdom born of experience, Edith knew Rosamund wanted to talk—indeed, would talk when she was ready.

Meantime, Edith's thoughts had been traveling along old pathways. Rosamund's uncanny likeness to her mother put the reminiscing woman in an odd place, one which only old people know. Somehow the past and the present ran together here and there like berry dye in a vat of whites.

Finally, Rosamund's wistful words broke the sound barrier. "Edith. . ." She faltered and then continued, "will you tell me about my mother?" The precious word fell softly from her lips.

Edith looked up from the heap of herb stalks mounded at her feet, paused in her work, and further scrunched up her wrinkled face in consideration before she replied, "Why, dearie! There's nothin' I'd rather be talkin' about!"

She paused, as though sorting memories piece by piece. "English, she was. And, oh, so pretty!" Craning her neck, her faded blue eyes looked through Rosamund as though seeing someone else. "Her picture ye be, my dear." She blinked and gave a little jerk. Her head bobbed and she resumed snapping herb leaves from their stalks.

Rosamund wondered if Edith would say any more, but after a lengthy period of silence, without even looking up, she continued in her own roundabout way. "Your papa be meetin' her first, he did. Seems 'twas on one of them there tradin' trips. Ya, ya. He went with my Lord Schmidden—his papa. 'Twould be your grandpapa, now wouldn't it?"

Obviously not expecting a reply from Rosamund, she mused on, "Smitten, he was!" She grinned an almost toothless grin and waggled her head. Frizzy gray hair, what there was of it, only added to her wizened appearance. "Never have I seen a lad so besotted! Ach! Quite off his head, I tell ye."

Her thoughts focused more clearly, and she reminisced volubly. "When plans be set for the weddin' he flashed about like a courtin' grouse. Burg Mosel saw the scrubbin' of all time; Master Klaus said things must be jes' right for to be bringin' home a bride—but he couldn't be seein' straight for to do a blessed thing!" She chuckled to herself. "And when the Lady Rose was come! Well, then we be understandin'! We took to her in a blink, even my Lady Clara—and a hard one to be pleasin', she was. And I should know! Twenty years I be workin' for my Lady."

Rosamund had forgotten her work, her hands resting idly on either side of the kettle in her lap. Bright eyes fixed on Edith, she absorbed every word.

Edith rambled on. "Lady Rose loved to ride, she did. And your papa, he be buyin' her a mare. Black it be, and shiny in the sun. She brushed it 'til I 'spected it's hair would be fallin' out for certain! Windy, she be callin' it. I heard tell your papa be up and sellin' her after your mama—"

Her words faded with her breath, and she stared at the fire, her lined face creasing into even deeper folds. After a moment she turned an intent look on Rosamund. "Pfeiffer, he's bein' Windy's colt. *You* be knowin' Pfeiffer?" she questioned, almost as if Pfeiffer were a person.

Rosamund murmured an assent, but Edith had already wandered aloud down another memory. "And the big singin' machine what Lady Rose be learnin' to play. And that Frenchman what be teachin' her, him's what be makin' eyes at my lady! I heard her tellin' him to be leavin' her alone—she what be lovin' Klaus an' all."

Rosamund froze. Stunned. But Edith, unaware that her disclosure was disconcerting, continued to ramble along her memories, and Rosamund had to scramble mentally to keep up with her.

"So kind, your mama. Always doin' for others. When my Lord and Lady took low with the black sickness, she said we must be lettin' her nurse them—seein' as they was like her own folks. Like that, she was. And when they both died, it went so hard she couldn't save them that we be fearin' for her."

Edith rubbed her bleary eyes with a gnarled, arthritic hand and sniffed unashamedly. "I thought belike she'd wear out a bench in the empty chapel, sittin'. Seems she needed somethin' what we couldn't be givin' her." Again retracing a trail of her own, she fell silent.

Rosamund's tears obscured her vision, and she blinked them down her rosy cheeks.

After a moment Edith's thoughts came back to the present, and she sighed. Watching Rosamund, the memories were strong indeed. "Your papa, dear boy, be worryin' hi'self to a shadow. He set to send her to the hot springs—but she wouldn't be havin' any of it. Stubborn girl she be, your mama. But we sure be lovin' her!"

Edith's mind went off on another tangent and Rosamund waited impatiently. Short bursts of conversation were tolerable for a few minutes, but finally she reached out and touched Edith's hand, bringing her back to the present. "And then what happened?" she whispered.

"Why, 'twas the strangest thing ye ever did be tellin'. In one day she be her fair self again! Jes' like that! In fine fettle. We be most catched by wonderment."

"Yes?" Rosamund barely breathed the word lest she disturb Edith's memories.

"She said, sure an' I'm sittin' here, that God spoke to her! I don't rightly mind how that could be. God never spoke to me, nor anybody's I be knowin'. But belike 'twas a dream or a vapor. Naught of us be knowin'—but we was gladdened for certain to be havin' our dear Rose back."

Rosamund's eyes grew wide as realization struck her. Rose, her own precious mother, had come to know God like she had! Her heart gave a great leap within her. But

Edith continued, unaware of Rosamund's inner excitement, "Then you were on the way, and I know'd I'se bein' too old to be nursin' ye. That's when I be comin' here—where I growed up, you know."

Edith laid aside her pot of herbs, rose, and shuffled over to the fireplace. She ladled up a bowl of stew for each of them out of the kettle perpetually suspended to one side in the fireplace pit. "It's sure to be gettin' colder, Rose." She called her by her mother's name, as though they were one and the same. "The flames be 'comin' blue. It's to stop snowin', it is." She leaned into the door and slowly heaved it open. True to her prediction the wind had died down and snow no longer fell, and although she had barely opened the door for a peek, snow cascaded inside from the drift deposited against it like a homeless vagabond.

Edith whisked up the rapidly melting snow, her mind still on their earlier conversation. "Your mama loved the snow, she did. She'd go trampin' in it, be makin' trails with her little feet. Then your papa, he'd be followin' her trails to find her. Laugh, they would, when he'd be findin' her! It was a game, she said."

The two women, the old one and the young one, resumed their industry. For that is what it was. Edith garnered herbs, far more than she needed for her own purposes. Then each year at the village fair she bartered her herbs for goods provided by other villagers as well as itinerant fair merchants who followed the trade route and stopped at many small villages along the way. They came each year, bringing news and merchandise.

Rosamund's father had himself made many trips over the years along the trade route. He'd be gone for several months at a time and return with crates full of marvelous finds, some useful and some not so useful—like Beenie, the pet monkey, who drove everyone crazy with his chatter and littering! Young Rosamund had loyally defended him. And no one had quite had the heart to rejoice when poor Beenie drowned in a horse trough.

Several times Rosamund had begged to accompany her father on a trip, but he always insisted that traveling wasn't safe for pretty little girls. So she'd had to content herself with his stories and gifts and her own vivid imagination.

Rosamund continued to work the herbs, but often she would scoop up the leaves already heaped in her kettle and let them trickle slowly through her fingers. Like her thoughts. Edith sagely observed this preoccupation, and she waited. Her homely intuition proved right, and Rosamund voiced a second question. "Edith, did anyone ever—that is, were you ever very fond of someone? A man, I mean." She hid her eyes behind long lashes that brushed her pink-stained cheeks.

Edith wanted to laugh and cry at the same time. Laugh, because Rosamund was yet so delightfully sweet and innocent. Cry, because she remembered when Lord Schmidden had asked her a similar question. Ensuing love had brought him supreme joy and intense anguish. And now his Rosamund teetered on the threshold of *her* future. The girl's face betrayed her heart, and Edith wondered if love would bring her happiness or sorrow. However, she kept these thoughts to herself.

Instead, she answered Rosamund's hesitant question, "Ach, my lady. Pleasin' to the eyes I be once. Ye'd never think it to be lookin' at me now." Her hunched shoulders quaked with her mirth. "Near ready for the hereafter, I am!" She pinched a prune-wrinkled cheek. "My birthin' sack's quite ripe, so 'tis!"

Rosamund raised her dark brows over eyes filled with amazement. Never had she known anyone so odd as Edith.

"There be two young men what set store by me, they did. I had to be choosin'. Richard Schwartz, him it was what be pesterin' the patience out o' me. He'd got hi'self the best prospects, he did, but he wouldn't be takin' kindly to hearin' no for ought. He'd be gettin' angered easy and blamin' everybody less hi'self." She eyed Rosamund with a cunning look the girl had never seen her wear before. "I 'spected if I be choosin' him, he'd be angered at me the most 'cause I'd be in his door, comin' and goin'!"

Her head bobbed several times as if to affirm her conclusion before she continued, "And then there be Alfie Baer." She said his name again, "Alfie," slowly and dreamily, as if she were in the throes of first love. "Him it be 'twas sweet on me. His big brown eyes would be meltin' my heart jes' like that there snow, so's I could hardly be breathin'."

Edith's faded eyes lit up just thinking about him and Rosamund listened with her mouth slightly open, drinking in the words she thirsted to hear.

Edith drew her shriveled self up proudly, lifted her ample chin, and with a preening motion she smoothed a gnarled, brown-spotted hand over her cheek and ear. As if she were still young and beautiful, she said proudly, "So I be choosin' Alfie!"

After a pause, Edith continued her musing, "Richard

said I'd be livin' in regrets. Later he be marryin' to Gertie Lund; she be havin' an eye for nice things. But I heard tell he'd beat her betimes. I be guessin' what there be things more 'portant in life than good prospects, and I never was regrettin' my choosin' Alfie. He didn't never get so fixed with earth's possessions, but his be a kind heart in his breast. So happy, we was. He wast be gone now for many a year, but my lovin' him jes' never dies. Him's still been livin' in my heart to this 'ere very day."

Edith stared into the fire, forgetful of her guest, alone with memories only she could see, and Rosamund sat motionless, unwilling to disturb the musing old woman. She wished to consider what she'd just heard, and it seemed natural that her thoughts were drawn to Eric. His blue eyes had certainly taken her breath away! And she knew from past experience that he was thoughtful and kind. But still the question came: how do you know someone is right for you? It seemed such a risk. Your choice would affect the rest of your life. What if Edith had chosen Richard? What if you weren't even given a choice? She knew that was often the situation. What then?

The old woman gave a little bounce on the bench, and her words interrupted Rosamund's thoughts. "Ach, I jes' be seein' the past, dearie. Maybe you'st be seein' the future, ya?"

Rosamund blushed in startled confusion and looked away from Edith's knowing gaze. Her eyes came to rest on the enameled chest that had belonged to her mother. *Later,* she thought, *I'll get out the book and read a bit. Maybe God will speak to me again.* She glanced back at Edith and smiled shyly for her answer. They continued working with the herbs. Quiet. Content.

Later that evening when steady, deep snoring confirmed Edith's sound sleep and held promise of solitude, Rosamund slipped from the straw bed and knelt beside the waiting chest. Carefully, quietly, she opened the heavy lid. This time, without pausing, she quickly drew out the contents, intent on only one thing—the book. Holding it firmly in her grasp—and after a hasty glance to be sure Edith was still sleeping—she curled up on the floor beside the bench and tucked her stockinged feet under the skirt of her nightdress. She unlatched the clasp and opened the cover in tense anticipation. Carefully she placed the yellow rose on the bench beside her.

Hour One began, *Blessed is the man. . . No, that's not what I'm looking for; I'm not a man!* she thought impatiently, turning several pages. She paused at Hour Four. Tipping the book so the firelight could shine on the page, she read:

> The Lord is my shepherd;
>   I shall not want.
> He maketh me to lie down in green pastures:
>   He leadeth me beside the still waters.
> He restoreth my soul:
>   He leadeth me in the paths of righteousness
> For his name's sake.
> Yea, though I walk
>   Through the valley of the shadow of death,
> I will fear no evil:
>   For thou art with me;
> Thy rod and thy staff
>   They comfort me.

Thou preparest a table before me
In the presence of mine enemies:
Thou anointest my head with oil;
My cup runneth over.
Surely goodness and mercy shall follow me
All the days of my life:
And I will dwell in the house of the Lord
For ever.
—Psalm 23

The words were alive—she could reach out and press them in the palm of her hand. The sense of God's presence swept over her, and this time she recognized it instantly. The breathless warmth reached to her toes and a sweet perfume seemed to scent the air. Galloping with Pfeiffer, as fast as he could carry her, had dulled the lonely ache for a time, but this was different. That place of pain no longer hurt. It hadn't, she realized, since that recent night when God's presence had cradled her. Baby-soft fresh pink skin covered the old wound. Healing had blotted up yesterday's sorrow. The haunting shadows of the past tormented no more. Yesterday and her mother both belonged to God. She felt healthy. Whole. Safe in God's care.

She read it again, *He leadeth me in the paths of righteousness. . .* "Oh!" She paused, seeing meaning beyond the mere words. "God will guide me."

I will fear no evil: for thou art with me. "God will be with me—and with Papa, too, please!" she hastened to add.

Through the mist in her eyes she made out the next words and read softly under her breath, "Surely goodness and mercy shall follow me all the days of my life: and I will dwell in the house of the Lord for ever."

Leaning her elbow on the bench, she propped her chin in her hand as she mused over the meaning of the words. Yes, she understood! God's presence would always be with her, and He would take care of the future. Rosamund had found that place of quiet rest near God's heart.

The temperature outside continued to drop, and eventually the chill of the room registered in her consciousness. With a little shiver she slipped the yellow rose back inside the front of the book, refastened the heavy clasp, and hastily wrapped it again in its silk scarf. She fitted it back into the bottom of the chest and then replaced the other keepsakes. Gently, quietly, she eased down the heavy enameled lid until she heard the spring click shut.

Rosamund slipped back into bed and snuggled down between the goose down comforters that covered the straw. Drifting off to sleep, her thoughts returned to Edith's comment earlier in the day: *His eyes would be meltin' my heart, jes' like that there snow—so's I could hardly be breathin'*. Somehow she couldn't help but think of Eric's blue eyes.

nine

Eric stood alone on the walking edge of the wide stone wall. He placed his elbows on the ledge of a tapering recess, one of many arrow loops designed into the wall to protect sentries and provide visibility, and leaned out to view the whitewashed landscape encircling Burg Mosel. Frosted trees whiskered the distant rolling hills, and curling tendrils of village smoke rose upward in clusters spotted here and there over the countryside.

Eric's crew, sharpening their battle skills, were engaged in target practice in the stable yard, and Eric could hear their shouts—like background music for his thoughts.

Eric recalled his contact seven years ago with Lord Schmidden and Rosamund. The design of Feste Burg, the Schmidden's military outpost along the coast, definitely suited its purpose, but it had represented Eric's only tangible association with the nobleman and his daughter.

Now the grandeur of Burg Mosel gave him a new awareness of their impressive heritage. Many of the rooms were filled with imported treasures, and Eric marveled that a girl like Rosamund, accustomed to such fineness, could have been so at home in Edith's poor cottage. Instead of casting a shabby frown on the humble dwelling, her very presence had seemed to glorify its simplicity.

Her sweet delight in finding God through the pages of her book rose to the fore of his thoughts. An ache filled his heart, a yearning that never stayed silent for long. He let his mind picture his dreams as reality. Surely she embodied all the virtues he had idealized over the years: beauty, grace, a quick mind, gentle ways, and a nature sensitive to God. Had anyone ever been so perfect for him?

Almost, he had decided to speak to Lord Schmidden, but after the tour of Burg Mosel and recalling his status as a guest—and a foreigner at that—he'd thought better of his foolhardy impulse. His neck grew hot just thinking about the rejection his impertinence would likely bring him. Certainly Lord Schmidden would have already carefully arranged or, at the least, made definite plans for his only child's future.

To force himself to redirect his thoughts, Eric began to walk around the top of the castle wall. He gazed out at the snow-covered fields, the twisting frozen river, and the winding pathway that led down from the grand stone fortress at the summit where he stood. It all served to impress upon him the gulf between himself and Lord Schmidden's beloved daughter. To hope was to look at that for which he would never presume to ask.

Contrasting his lowly station to Rosamund's noble status made him turn away from the open sky and plunge determinedly into the dark tunnel of steps that wound down to the courtyard below. He must discard his dreams, purge them from his heart even as a doctor would purge bad blood. To dream of what he could not have would only keep him from fulfilling his purpose here. He knew he would have to subjugate his thoughts once and for all if he truly meant to do his duty and depart with self-respect. He groaned. Making noble decisions was easy, but living them out required calling up the deepest resources of his soul.

Coming out into the sunshine at the bottom of the stairwell, Eric encountered Lord Schmidden. His recent thoughts tied up his tongue, but Lord Schmidden greeted him with pleasure, completely unaware of Eric's inner struggle.

"Oh, there you are, Branden. I want to review with you the weapons we have in storage. I asked Curtis to show you around." He paused as though waiting for Eric's response.

"He did. Thank you, sir." Eric replied respectfully.

Lord Schmidden talked while they walked across the gravel yard bordered on two sides by the stables. A hedge separated the stable yard from the garden on the third side.

"I really don't know what we'll find in the armory. There hasn't been a need to defend ourselves for nearly a hundred years, and I've had no interest in fighting, even for sport. Everything will probably be quite antiquated. But we can acquire whatever you feel is needed."

When they reached the building he had referred to as the armory, Lord Schmidden drew an iron key from his pouch and inserted it into the keyhole. It grated as it turned. With a thrust of his shoulder that caused the door to bend before it gave way, Lord Schmidden pushed it open and stood aside for Eric to precede him into the dim, musty room. They stepped inside and waited momentarily while their eyes adjusted to the gloom.

A quick inventory revealed a heap of mismatched pieces of steel armor including leg pieces piled against the back wall, several helmets with rusted visors hanging on wooden pegs, and an odd assortment of deteriorating leather vests lying in the right front corner. A dozen or so maces were scattered about on the floor in a disorderly fashion, and a row of swords, sabers, and lances, two dozen at the most, were hanging on one wall.

A closer review told Eric that only eight of the swords were sheathed in scabbards and the lot were in sore need of honing. Their usefulness was uncertain at best. Even in the dim light it was obvious that no formidable cache of weapons had been stored here.

The dinner bell clanged. At the timely interruption Lord Schmidden ruefully pinched his lower lip and commented with a wry smile, "Well, Branden, let's go eat. We'll talk about weapons later on a full stomach!"

ten

The sky shone May-blue, and a few cottontail clouds puffed up here and there. Wildflowers nodded their bright heads and whispered nuances of sweet aroma to the wind. Trees were fresh with mint green leaves and distant amethyst mountains lifted still-white peaks in worship. It was a perfect day for a fair!

A gentle breeze wafted in through the open door, and prisms of sunlight played hopscotch on the floor of Edith's cottage. Edith bent over the sleeping girl. Dark hair curled around her shoulders, and one bare foot peeked out from under the bed covering.

"Come, come, child!" Edith gave her guest a wake-up call.

Opening one eye, Rosamund stared up at Edith as though her spirit were returning from a distant place. She rolled over and sat up, stretching slender arms above her head. "Today is the day!" she exclaimed, realizing the day of the fair had arrived at last.

Springing up from the low bed, she caught Edith's hands and pulled her into a nimble quickstep, the two of them whirling about in the warm sunshine. Round and round they went. Rosamund's nightdress ballooned out like a church bell pealing its call, and Edith's shapeless frock twisted tighter and tighter around her lumpy shape until her aged body betrayed her willing spirit and she tripped over her own feet. Rosamund caught her, and they clung to each other, laughing with abandon like two giddy school girls.

"Go on wi' ye!" Edith tried to sound severe as she pushed unruly hair away from her face, but their eyes met and the laughter began all over again.

Rosamund slipped hastily out of her nightdress and into Kathe's well-worn frock, preoccupied with Edith's explanation of the village fair. "We be workin' all the winter for this day. Seems each of us villagers needs be havin' somethin' to keep our hands agoin' so's we be livin' to see the spring. Tradin' our doin's is such a merriment—and of certain there'll be a smattering of merchants what be comin' in on the trade route. Certain of them be comin' every year. Like Ol' Robert, what be makin' shoes. And Limpin' George, what be sellin' knives, swords, and weapons-like; he ain't never missed a spring fair since what I be livin' here, and nigh on to twenty years that be!"

Hurrying to accommodate Edith's impatience, Rosamund followed her out the door and down the hard-packed path toward the village center. Barnyard smells tweaked their noses, and the din of activity could be heard immediately: animals baaing and braying, poultry cackling and squawking, and even the voice of a recalcitrant pig squealed intermittently above the rest. Villagers spilled out of their doors, braced, armed, pulling, encumbered with all sorts of strange and unwieldy appendages—and Rosamund and Edith blended into the scene.

Rosamund walked demurely beside Edith. She held the handle on her side of the large woven basket between

them and listened as Edith called a greeting to this one
and that; she smiled and nodded to those who included
her in their friendly hellos.

The predictably quiet village had become a teeming
marketplace. Booths, each a board balanced on a pair of
homely sawhorses and shaded by a canopy of cloth
rigged over a simple frame, stood around the perimeter
of the village center. Here and there animals were teth-
ered to spikes or posts, and villagers and itinerant merchants did their best to display their wares to greatest
advantage.

During the housebound days of winter, Edith and
Rosamund had torn a large piece of muslinlike cloth
into many pieces, each about a handbreadth square.
Mounding a handful of garnered herbs in the center of
each square, they had pulled up the four corners and
created "pouches" which they had tied shut with cord.

Edith spread a bright blue length of cloth over their
table and suggested Rosamund arrange an appealing
display of the little herb bags. She handed Rosamund
the pouches, two at a time, visiting all the while with
passersby. "Good mornin' to ye, Frau Lanz!" she greeted
heartily, her double chin keeping time with her busy
mouth. "A right beautiful day it be, ya?"

"Morning, morning! That it be." Frau Lanz responded.

When she had passed on by, trailed by four young
children of varying sizes, Edith whispered to Rosamund,
quite loudly, the girl thought, "Looks like they be all
feelin' quite well ag'in. Mind you, if she be makin' those
young'ns to be wearin' undervests, they wouldna be gettin' the croup. Iffen ye be dressin' too light, ye be gettin'
a chill." She shook her head disparagingly. "But there be

some people what jes' won't be listenin', no how."

Rosamund continued arranging herb pouches while she listened to the conversations taking place around her. She knew the villages near Burg Mosel held annual fairs, and Kathe had told her snatches of the fun that occurred at such events. But Papa had dissuaded her when, on one occasion, she had wanted to accompany Hildy and Kathe. So today she had every pore open, absorbing village life with all five senses. Indeed, some of the smells were unpleasant, and the heat, dirt, and noise were unlike anything she had ever experienced. But the delight she felt at just being a part was so intense that the distasteful aspects hardly merited passing consideration.

Her cheeks glowed with excitement, and her eyes danced about, trying to take in every detail. Kathe's shabby frock was unable to conceal her loveliness, and many a villager turned for a second look at the pretty girl assisting old Mother Baer. The moisture of youth had been wrung from Edith in the inevitable progression from mortality to eternity, and the young and the old worked side by side in vivid contrast.

When all the pouches were satisfactorily displayed, Edith left Rosamund to tend the booth alone while she made the rounds. "Be havin' a look-see," she said.

Nobody bartered much early on. Folk moved about from booth to booth, greeting each other, discussing the weather, the husband, the wife, the children, Aunt Millie, the lame cow, the tabby cat's new kittens. They laughed and joked, admired each other's wares, and enjoyed the day as if it were a holiday.

The out-of-town merchants had no lack of business.

People queued at Ol' Robert's booth to be sized for shoes. Mamas and papas with a stair step of children at their heels stood in the warm sunshine, awaiting their turn. Womenfolk clustered around the booth that displayed large spools of brightly colored fabric which contrasted with their dull homespun; it awakened an appreciation for beauty in some and stirred up dissatisfaction in others. And Limpin' George was surrounded by men discussing the latest inventions in weaponry.

Socialization, this important aspect of village life, intrigued Rosamund. She had always lived a somewhat isolated existence, and Edith, aware of that fact, watched from a distance as her charge blossomed. Shyly at first and then more confidently, Rosamund participated in conversation with the visitors to their booth.

In the late morning, Edith returned to the booth and insisted that Rosamund take a turn visiting other booths. Seven-year-old Sarah, one of Frau Lanz's daughters, had taken a liking to Rosamund and offered to accompany her, so the two set off together, a hot, chubby hand enclosed in a slender, cool one.

In the center of the village square, surrounded by the merchant booths, a running program of spontaneous entertainment amused the patrons of the fair. Sarah tugged at Rosamund's hand, insisting they go to see the "ball-man." A puzzled and apologetic Rosamund followed in Sarah's anxious wake as she wormed her way through the crowd that had gathered to watch a jolly juggler demonstrate his skill.

His exhibition was followed by the performance of a painted-face mime. He stood perfectly still while only his eyes moved; he rolled them about in exaggerated movements, winking deliberately and elaborately at various ladies in the crowd. They blushed and looked away, or clucked their tongues to disguise pleasure or express disgust. The mime winked at little Sarah and she burst into delighted giggles. But when his eyes settled on Rosamund, who was standing quietly beside Sarah, and remained there, staring, Rosamund blushed uncomfortably. She pulled a protesting Sarah away through the crowd. Somehow she couldn't quite explain, even to herself, the tumult of her emotions.

By this time the sun shone directly overhead and many of the venders were eating provisions brought with them from home. Rosamund sank to the grass in relief as she and Sarah reached Frau Lanz's booth. Edith and Rosamund had joined the Lanz family, contributing black bread to the meal of goat cheese and plump red berries—berries that Sarah proudly announced she had picked "all myself!" They washed everything down with gulps of homemade tea of a nondescript variety shared from a common family jug and listened to Sarah's chatter about the "ball-man" and the "winker."

When the remains of lunch had been tidied up and put away, Rosamund stood, ready to move on again. Because it was Sarah's turn to help her mother with the care of the baby, Rosamund wandered on alone. She slipped in and out of clustered folk, absorbing the sights and sounds and trying to get close enough to see the goods proffered at each booth.

She paused to listen to the minstrel performing in the square; he sang a sad ballad of love and loss. Here and there, older couples listened as they stood close to each other. Some held hands. The younger ones laughed in giddy embarrassment as a boy or two tried to steal a kiss from a saucy maid. Rosamund smiled and turned away.

She visited politely with the proprietors of six or seven booths as she continued on her way around the square. For the moment, thoughts of Papa, of Eric, of Lord Frederick were forgotten. Rosamund looked around, completely relaxed and unwary in her happiness, and observed the bustling activity taking place under the blue sky with its soft mountains of drifting white clouds. Oh, never had there been a day more wonderful!

Taking a step, as if to continue on, she saw that Limpin' George's booth was next. A group of men stood in a knot at the front of the booth. In that instant she froze, rooted in dread. It couldn't be! Not on this bright, lilting day. No! No! She must be mistaken! But she wasn't. There, pressed about by village men, stood the handsome Lord Frederick and Louie, his stout administrator! The two men were obviously the focus of male attention and admiration.

Rosamund had little time to wonder at their purpose for being at the fair. She overheard the discussion, cuttingly distinct. "I've got a storeroom full of these." Lord Frederick held up a long sword. He drew the slick edge over his thumb and beads of warm blood popped out along the slice. Raising the sword high, he flashed it about. Its gleaming razored blade flashed deadly molten red in the sun. "I'll be making good use of them soon enough. My neighbor has been a continual source of irritation, quite an uncooperative fellow!"

Stunned silence fell over the onlookers until one of the village men questioned in awe, "Do you mean to attack him?"

"Certainly." Lord Frederick made the boast with a defiant raise of his handsome chin as he cut another hissing slash through the air with the bloodied sword. The men standing closest instinctively jumped back, startled. His bold dark eyes moved over them, feeding on their admiration and fear. "He's really no threat—just an unchallenged country yokel. I doubt he could muster five hundred men to resist me!"

Rosamund thought her heart would stop. That was *her papa* he was speaking of so disparagingly. But before her thoughts could progress, the stout overseer continued smugly, "An offer of marriage for his daughter he foolishly refused!"

Lord Frederick's eyes narrowed, and he frowned at Louie's indiscreet disclosure.

"All this for a wife!" another villager exclaimed. The ways of the wealthy were certainly past understanding. Before Lord Frederick could answer, Louie spoke out again with a smirk, not yet aware of Lord Frederick's disapproval, "It's his property we want, although the girl *is* a pretty little skirt."

The faces of the villagers reflected the tension on Lord Frederick's face, and Louie avoided Lord Frederick's eyes. Time would diminish Lord Frederick's irritation, and Louie would think up some justifiable excuse for his overactive tongue—beside the truth, that is. It would never do to admit his craving for admiration.

The men snickered, embarrassed at the unabashed vulgarity. Never did it enter their minds that Mother Baer's sweet Rosamund was the object of these men's greed.

Rosamund, however, had heard more than enough. Her cheeks burned, and hot sparks shot from her indignant blue eyes. She turned to run, but in her haste to escape she stumbled over the tether of somebody's goat. The fall brought her to her senses; she must not draw attention to herself! Chastened, she straightened up and made her way quietly back to the security of Edith and her herb booth.

Although Rosamund valiantly tried to hide her distress, a shrewd Edith noted her agitation and persistent watchfulness; however, she wisely let the girl keep her secret, and Rosamund gratefully accepted Edith's unquestioning support.

But if Rosamund's tongue remained still, her emotions cascaded violently over rocky thoughts. So, Lord Frederick *had* come to see her father. And he had asked to marry her. Instead of feeling flattered as she once would have, Rosamund shook with fury at even being found attractive by such a villainous character, and she felt personally defensive of her self-respect.

Whether it made matters better or worse, she wasn't quite sure, but to know Lord Frederick didn't really want her—that she just provided an avenue for him to take advantage of Papa—stung with the betrayal of a Judas kiss. Her naiveté had found Lord Frederick handsome and fascinating. Oh, the shame!

At last her father's bewildering distress of last fall made sense. Now she understood why he had so hopefully suggested she visit Edith. Her insides seethed with white-water anger, and several times the hissing boiled up until she had to clench one hand in the other to keep the tremors from betraying her internal agitation.

Lord Frederick and his administrator never passed by their booth, and that evening when Rosamund and Edith slowly wended their way homeward—Edith picking her way as if her feet knew every stick and stone—even in the darkness, Rosamund remained silent.

Edith immediately fell into an exhausted sleep, but in spite of the long, busy day, a troubled Rosamund couldn't seem to relax. She lay awake, thinking and worrying. Her thundering heart shook her whole body. Her head pounded. Like stinging nettles, the nerves in her arms and legs sabotaged sleep. She tossed and turned, trying to relieve the throbbing that knotted her stomach and choked off her breathing. But her pulse dominated every position.

Then it came to her. The book! She slipped stealthily from the bed, trying not to disturb Edith. Her hands shook as she touched the home-dipped candle close to the dying fireplace embers. Shading the fresh flame with her hand, she moved to place the candleholder on the floor between the little chest and the bed. She bit her lower lip between her teeth, concentrating on lifting the contents out of the chest, one at a time, until she again held the book in her anxious fingers. *How odd,* she thought, *that just holding the book brings comfort.*

Even though it had been generously warm in the daytime, Edith's cottage felt chilly at night without a fire, and Rosamund began to shiver. She hurried over to the bed and inched back under the comforter. Carefully, she opened the book's heavy clasp, lifted the ivory cover, and then placed the yellow rose on the floor beside the candleholder.

Her shaking fingers tried to turn the pages, but she lost her grip and the book slipped. With a smothered gasp and a quick movement, she caught it; she cast a nervous glance at Edith to be sure she was still asleep.

The book fell open to Hour Four. *I read that last time,* she thought, and quickly turned to the next page. Hour Five. The words were for her:

> The Lord is my light and my salvation;
>   Whom shall I fear?
> The Lord is the strength of my life;
>   Of whom shall I be afraid?
> When the wicked, even mine enemies and my foes,
>   Came upon me to eat up my flesh,
> They stumbled and fell.
>   Though an host should encamp against me,
> My heart shall not fear:
>   Though war should rise against me,
> In this will I be confident.

She continued reading to the final verses.

> I had fainted, unless I had believed
>   To see the goodness of the Lord
> In the land of the living.
>   Wait on the Lord:
> Be of good courage,
>   And he shall strengthen thine heart:
> Wait, I say, on the Lord.
> —Psalm 27

God's presence filled the room. Rosamund whispered softly, "The Lord is the strength of my life; of whom shall I be afraid?" She repeated it, "The Lord is the strength of my life; of whom shall I be afraid?" And again, "The Lord is the strength of my life. . ."

The shaking stopped. The throbbing eased. Her nerves calmed. Anxiety simply disappeared at the Word of the Lord. With a sigh of relief she slipped the yellow rose back inside the cover, closed the book gently, and laid it on the floor next to the candle. She snuffed out the flame and snuggled down under the comforter. Closing her eyes, she murmured again, "Of whom shall I be afraid?" The words faded into nothingness as she fell asleep.

ᴥ

Rosamund awoke the next morning to discover Edith sitting on the wooden threshold of the open cottage door. Her back rested against one side of the doorjamb and her knees were bent and her bare feet were placed, one on top of the other, against the base of the opposite side of the door frame. Rosamund had opened her lips to call out a "Good morning," but then she saw her mother's book, open and resting on Edith's lap. Dismay followed surprise. And then a rush of compassion and love flooded her heart. "Do you know what you're reading?" she gently questioned Edith.

Lost in her own thoughts, Edith did not apologize for having Rosamund's book. Instead, she lifted sad eyes and her despairing words echoed in the cottage. "I canna be readin' it. Naught what ever be learnin' me!"

Rosamund responded softly, "The book tells about God. I can read to you if you'd like."

The joy that flooded the old woman's face was pathetic to see. Rosamund got up and went over to sit beside her. She opened the book to the presentation page and read aloud her father's inscription, keeping her eyes fixed on the book as Edith tried to rub away the tears that ran down her shriveled face. Rosamund turned the pages rapidly. Even as she had first read the scribe's prayer at the end of the book, Rosamund read it now to Edith.

"Oh, my, but it's bein' so beautiful!" Edith exclaimed.

Turning to Hour Twelve, Rosamund repeated the words found in Psalm 63 which had first touched her own heart. "Oh God, thou art my God; early I seek thee. . ." God's presence flooded over both of them as Rosamund read the rest of the chapter, and Edith's hungry heart received His love and mercy in exchange for her fear and superstition.

"Oh! Oh! Oh!" she gasped again and again. Finally pure joy caused her to laugh. It bubbled up like an artesian spring.

The old woman's joy was infectious. Rosamund joined in the laughter and hugged Edith exuberantly. And the duties of the day became as play. First one and then the other would stop to say, "Let's read some more from the book." Sweet fellowship knit them together, for their hearts had found peace through God's Word.

eleven

The great room at Burg Mosel had undergone a major transformation. The elegant furniture and accessories had been removed to the adjoining music salon, and the heavy draperies formed a partition between the two rooms. Even though the windows stood open, the room reeked of unbathed bodies, and all other sounds seemed lost in the rattle of the clashing new swords that had replenished the armory. Eric had organized his crew members into a training team. Their goal was to sharpen the fighting skills of village men conscripted for preparation during the winter months in anticipation of a spring confrontation with Lord Frederick.

Eric looked up as Lord Schmidden entered the doorway of the great room. One of those men whose presence could be felt before he was seen, Lord Schmidden had been born to wealth and a position of authority. Nevertheless, the respect accorded him by his loyal subjects was deserved; he had been a kindly overseer yet a firm arbiter in matters of dispute.

Lord Schmidden, blue eyes keen under bushy brows, scanned the room until he located Eric; their eyes met. Lord Schmidden beckoned with a nod of his head for Eric to join him. Eric excused himself and wove his way through the gladiating men.

"How's it going, Branden?" Lord Schmidden questioned

when Eric stopped beside him.

"Very well, sir." Eric spoke loudly to be heard above the din of swords, groans, and the occasional expletive.

Lord Schmidden eyed the roomful of men grouped in pairs, each thrusting and sparring vigorously, and especially so with Lord Schmidden in their midst. Each wished to look his best.

"Step out here with me." The older man put a hand on Eric's shoulder, and they moved through the doorway, side by side. Although about the same height, Eric's well-built frame in no way threatened Lord Schmidden's powerful build. Halting in the corridor, Lord Schmidden questioned Eric more specifically about the military exercises.

With a gesture of his head toward the room they had just left, Eric responded, "The men you saw in there are the final division. We've exercised men from fourteen villages—a total of about fifteen hundred men. I've divided them into groups of archers, swordsmen, lancers on horseback, and those who will operate the catapults, cannons, and battering ram. Various members of my crew have been assigned as leaders for each group—and I'll bear the standard and signal directions."

Eric lowered his voice and turned his back to the doorway. It was his turn to question. "Have you any news of Lord Frederick? We've only got three days left until his deadline."

Lord Schmidden lowered his voice as well, "One of the scouts just reported back. Lord Frederick is mustering troops for an attack. The information I received indicated it would be within the week. Apparently, he's enlisted the aid of two neighboring landowners. It seems he is unaware of your presence here. My scout got the impression Lord Frederick doesn't feel I'm a particularly formidable foe. That must be why he sends Louie to deliver his threats. Anyhow, combined, he said they have no more than a thousand men—so *we* have the advantage there. Won't he be in for a nest-ruffling?"

Lord Schmidden continued, sober once again, "But we must move immediately if we expect our plans to succeed." He clapped Eric on the back, "Go ahead, Branden. Take it from here and keep me informed." He turned on his heel and was gone. His abruptness, Eric knew, betrayed his anxiety; normally Lord Schmidden eased smoothly in and out of conversations.

Eric returned to the great room and stood quietly for a moment while he observed the engagements of the men and his crew. He felt pleased with what he saw. Coming to a decision, he rang the bell to indicate he wished to make an announcement. "We'll be forming ranks tonight in the lower field. You are dismissed now to eat and get some rest. I'll see you at sundown. Karl and Olaf, may I speak to you privately?"

Following a short briefing, Karl and Olaf were dispatched to ride through the countryside with the rallying cry for the groups of village men who had returned to their homes after completing their session of training exercises. They would be expected to join Eric immediately.

Eric awoke with the first light of dawn. He lay on the hard earth, silently reflecting on the past day and a half. The men had met in the field that first night. After assigning them, according to their divisions, to various sites for sleeping, he had suggested everyone take the opportunity to get a good rest. He knew the night would not be without difficulty. Fear and excitement would do their best to keep the men awake, himself included.

An offensive attack had been decided upon, and yesterday's march had proceeded according to plan. They had followed the river, staying to the right bank. Moving nearly fifteen hundred men plus supplies proved a massive operation, and Eric felt grateful for adequate time to maneuver into a position that would place them at an advantage. He recalled his surprise that there had been no scouts or activity in evidence once they crossed over into enemy territory. Of course, Lord Frederick's land that extended up and out from the river *was* densely forested, and if he rallied troops, they would come from villages farther south and east. Still, Eric felt wary. Things seemed too quiet.

He had slept fitfully this second night; he was worried. Not as another in his place would have been—he had no doubts about his mission and he felt quite certain of his strategy—but with deep concern for the men under his command and the families each represented. He closed his eyes and repeated the Lord's Prayer, requesting divine assistance:

> Our Father
>   Which art in heaven,
> Hallowed be thy name.
>   Thy kingdom come.
> Thy will be done in earth,
>   As it is in heaven.
> Give us this day our daily bread.
>   And forgive us our debts,

As we forgive our debtors.
  And lead us not into temptation,
But deliver us from evil:
  For thine is the kingdom, and the power,
And the glory, for ever.

"And Lord, today especially, Your will be done, and I humbly request that You give us strength and wisdom. Amen."

Eric rose and gave orders for everyone to prepare to move while it was still early and cool. Steamy morning mist rose from the river. It hovered in thick silence that blanketed the surrounding lowland, muffling sound and providing the men with a measure of cover. It was a sign to Eric that God was with him.

Each unit waited in readiness while Eric rode review. Those on horseback, one hundred twenty of them, took the position of vanguard. Dressed in full white armor: breastplates, shields, arm-plates, leg-plates, and plumed helmets, each made of polished steel, the mounted unit sat proudly on powerful steeds. Bright banners of blue and white, carried high, proclaimed their presence to the rest of the company. Immediately behind them came the archers wearing link mail and headgear, their bows in hand and their arrows slung over their backs. They were followed by similarly dressed foot soldiers, equipped with swords and maces. Bringing up the rear were men assigned to the baggage train.

Eric took his place in front, his bright blue banner fanning out behind him as he rode. A commanding figure, he inspired the respect and devotion of those he led. He turned his head to look back on the impressive entourage under his authority. Mute expectancy ruled every face, and a terrible silence filled the air. The thrill of a challenge shot through Eric's veins—something he'd not felt in a long time. Indeed, he had the sense that they pursued a holy mission.

Slowly, deliberately, they began the move to cover the final distance.

Because surprise was the key element in Eric's strategy, when Lord Frederick's castle came into view on the hill in the distance, Eric signaled deployment with his blue banner. A crew set to work to assemble the catapult and battering ram, and each unit maneuvered into its predetermined position. When everything stood ready, Eric raised his sword high.

The stillness was ripped to shreds. Cannons spewed out flames and smoke. Their shuddering thunder caused the earth to shake. Towers and walls disappeared in banks of billowing smoke that hung motionless in the dead air. The die had been cast. Eric spurred his horse to a gallop, and the men on horseback followed his lead. Archers swarmed the hill. Bows twanged. Arrows whistled. Excitement surged to fever pitch. A forest of lances and banners approached toward the drawbridge. Foot soldiers grunted and groaned as they worked together to maneuver the catapult.

There was no response to this aggressive attack, and a dreadful thought clutched at Eric's brain. Could Lord Frederick have set out for Burg Mosel by another route?

But no! Shortly, sentries began returning fire from the walls. Missiles whizzed by the soldiers, whining through the air and knocking up the dirt where they struck. The drawbridge was lowered and men, like ants, streamed through the gate. Armed and armored they came, straight into battle with a waiting confrontation of lances and arrows. The drawbridge was immediately raised, which prevented Eric's men from entering the fortress and thereby securing an almost certain victory for Lord Frederick.

Eric's crew had trained the village men well, and each unit followed its leader. Eric observed the exchange of fire in satisfaction. But when the leader of the left wing of foot soldiers was wounded, Eric rode over and dismounted. He handed the flag to his page and rallied the men around himself, ordering them to follow him. They did, all four hundred of them.

He led them eastward up the slopes of the hill toward the fortress. Fierce and bloody battling ensued. Shouts, groans, and curses filled the air and added to the confusion. Man against man, hand-to-hand, with swords, maces, lances, arrows. Horses were felled here and there, neighing miserably. Wounded men gritted their teeth and went on fighting if they were able. It was better to be half-dead and standing than to be trampled to death underfoot.

The artillery duel continued, each side hammering away with all its might. A minute lasted a lifetime. The sun peaked and then began its descent. Lower and lower it sank in the sky as the long hours passed in a terrible battle marked by streaming bright flags, bursts of red fire, and gushes of white smoke—all stark against the gray sky.

Blood, sweat, and dirt mingled on each face, but the fierceness in the eyes told the tale. Cries and howls rent the air. Foot soldiers fought like a raging tide of destruction. Spears and swords shone with the gleam of the setting sun's searing flame. Accompanying the turmoil, the deafening yells of the archers could be heard, each sending his messengers of flying fire up, up, and over the wall. The banners of the horsemen were countless, blue and white clashing against the black and red, their accompanying lances driving wildly to unseat a foe.

When at last, out of the near-darkness, a shout rang out from the walls above, bearers of the black and red straggled back in disorder—and the blue and white went right along with them. Hacking. Lunging. Stabbing. Over mangled bodies, foot by foot, Eric's men pushed Lord Schmidden's enemies into the fortress.

The time had come for regrouping. Eric quickly withdrew and returned to his page. He raised a signal. Immediately, his soldiers turned their attention to the wounded; bearers of the blue and white were carried down the slopes and laid out in rows to be tended to as quickly and mercifully as possible. The dead were placed side by side, and men were set to digging graves. No one would suffer the indignity of a night without burial.

Lord Frederick's men were left where they had fallen; the shadowy hillside was strewn with wasted bodies. It was a sickening sight. The blood. The mutilations. The dead faces. Blank eyes staring out in wretched ghastliness.

Those not involved in caring for the wounded or burying the dead were again divided into units and deployed around the fortress. Darkness overtook them. The final count came to twelve dead, one hundred eighty-seven wounded, and eight missing, presumably within the castle walls. Four hundred sixty-two of Lord Frederick's fallen men were even yet lying on the slopes about the fortress; a significant loss for the black and red.

Food and sleep were now paramount—sunrise would bring another bloody day. Finally, a watch was posted from each division, and everyone else sought rest.

Eric awoke on the morning of the third day, bruised and sore from having slept in his armor. His thoughts took a philosophical turn as he reflected on the previous day's battle. It seemed in every war each side was convinced that God was on their side. Right or wrong, only one side could win. It was God who would decide, not according to right or wrong, but to bring about the purposes of His divine will. *So then*, Eric mused, *what is my responsibility in this?*

Quietly, into Eric's spirit, came the answer. *It is for you to follow your conscience, but it is God who will determine the final outcome. If you do what you know to be right, you can trust God with the consequences.*

"Oh Lord, the battle is Yours," he whispered the prayer. Then, inhaling deeply of fresh morning air, Eric stood confidently to his feet. Confidence, he discovered, comes from doing what you know is right.

And so began a new day. As soon as it was light, Eric sent runners to the various divisions to inform them of the day's strategy. When each unit responded in readiness, he nodded to the trumpeter, who signaled the attack. Lord Frederick's men had been watching. Once again the drawbridge was lowered, but this time Eric's men were ready.

Before Lord Frederick's men could get through the gate and onto the bridge, several of Eric's men had already braved the moat and were scrambling up from below. Unnoticed by the enemy, they quickly cut through the heavy ropes that raised and lowered the drawbridge. This opened the way for a frontal attack with the main gate as the target. The battering ram stood ready. The catapult waited.

Eric gave a signal with the banner. The battering ram rolled into place and began its bludgeoning business. It lunged forward and backed up to lunge again. Forward and back. Forward and back. Pounding away with all the strength of thirty-six work-hardened men.

Within minutes the wall walks teemed with soldiers who dumped bucketfuls of stones down on the men working the battering ram below. Eric's archers and cannoneers picked them off as rapidly as they could. Others dumped burning debris out through the machicolations, and Eric posted guards to call out warnings so his men could retreat in time to prevent injuries.

A second signal went up, and the catapult and cannons moved into action. The first shot of the catapult did very little damage. The men reloaded it and then stood at attention, waiting for Eric's signal.

The battering ram pounded repeatedly on the heavy doors as the process of assault continued. Back up. Re-engage. Propel. Impact!

Finally, when it seemed the doors had begun to weaken, Eric realized the men operating the ram verged on collapse. At his nod, the trumpeter blew the signal and a second crew leaped forward to replace the weary men. At long last the heavy doors shuddered and groaned. Iron bracings ripped loose from the doors with the shrill scream of metal being torn away from wood. A fierce and deafening roar of elation arose from the soldiers. Victory would be theirs!

When the doors gave way, the men operating the battering ram quickly backed it out of the way and foot soldiers streamed into the castle. At a signal, the catapult let fly again. The shot tore a hole in the bridge, cutting off traffic between the fortress and the surrounding countryside. The next shot of the catapult smashed into three of Lord Frederick's horsemen who appeared in the main gate, and this set the stage for the last furious struggle.

Slipping and sliding over the dead beneath their feet, the blue and white drove back the despairing forces of the black and red, cutting them down by the score. Cannon shots sparked a fire within the fortress. The wind had come up, quite unnoticed until it whipped the flames about in a frenzy, causing them to spread like wild fire. The acrid smoke that poured up and out in black billows coupled with the leaping scarlet flames could be seen for miles around—like a bloody gash in the early gray sky.

Fire and smoke snaked about those still fighting inside the castle. Friend and foe alike began to swarm up and over the walls. Scaling ladders were dropped on the outside, and men streamed down, choking and coughing. Eric had joined the foot soldiers in their press into the fortress, and now, like the others driven by the smoke, he made his way down a scaling ladder. Hampered by heavy steel armor and moving very slowly, a vengeful arrow caught him between his leg-plates.

Olaf, directly below him on the ladder, saw the arrow pierce his flesh. Panic surged through him as he realized that if Eric so much as moved, the arrow would break off in his body. After shouting desperately to Eric to hold tight, Olaf clenched his jaws and mustered every ounce of his strength to pull himself back up the several rungs separating them.

He clung to the ladder with one hand, swaying with it as men above and below continued to make their way down. With the other hand he reached up to seize the arrow sticking out of Eric's flesh, pulling it out with a decisive jerk. Olaf gasped in surprise—it was only a wooden practice arrow, not a deadly barbed metal arrow! In that moment he realized that Lord Frederick's men were nearly out of arrows.

The shock of the pain that tore through Eric temporarily disoriented him, and he lost his grip. Down, down, he went, crashing into the moat. Shouts went up from those soldiers who were close by, and several of them leaped into the water to pull their leader, heavy armor and all, up the side and onto dry ground. He lay there, coughing and choking on a mouthful of the foul water. Involuntarily, he clutched at his burning leg. Someone pushed through the gathered crowd and applied a dressing of salt and olive oil to the bloody, gaping wound and wrapped a rude bandage around Eric's leg to hold the dressing in place.

Eric wasted no time in self-pity or regret. Taking a strong breath and collecting his wits, he whistled sharply for his horse. His page came running up with his mount and the standard. "Give me the banner! Signal a retreat!" Eric commanded decisively. The young fellow handed Eric the blue-and-white flag, and the trumpeter raised the trumpet to his lips and blew a shrill blast. Instantly, Eric's men rallied, reassembling in their units.

Once more Eric signaled an attack. Those of Lord Frederick's men fortunate enough to still be alive now rued their station outside the burning fortress. Eric's men fell with renewed vigor on those who tried to escape.

Fighting step by step, to a man, the enemy was cut down.

A shout went up; wave after wave of loud cheering. The countryside reverberated with cries of victory. Eric's heart leaped within him. God had fought for him and answered his prayer. And he had fulfilled his vow to his friend.

Eric ordered his page to signal regrouping, and the men fell back into their units. Following a quick head count, a report was made to Eric. God be praised! The months of training had paid off in *living* flesh! Only thirty-seven dead. Two hundred forty-three were wounded. Twelve were missing. Each able man provided assistance for the wounded and did his duty by the dead. Signs of scorching destruction still floated in the air, and smoke continued to rise from the ruins, filling the air with a dreadful stench, but by the time everyone had reassembled, all that remained of Lord Frederick's castle was a charred, smoldering shell containing the remains of its overly ambitious lord.

Gingerly, Eric mounted his horse. He signaled and there followed a loud blast on the trumpet. The blue banner waved triumphantly as Eric led the march toward home. Good news he would bear to Lord Schmidden!

twelve

It was midmorning of the next day before they began moving. The early sun shone through the tattered canopy of clouds and burned away the mist that draped the hills. The village men had been released to return to their homes, and Eric's crew, with great spirit, sang as they marched the final distance toward Burg Mosel. Eric's wound throbbed painfully, but he knew a report to Lord Schmidden must come first—before personal concerns. Leaving Olaf in charge of the slow-moving procession, he headed for the castle alone.

He rode around to the stables at the back, slid off his mount, threw the reigns over the horse's head, and limped across the stable yard and then along the hedge to the back doors of the entrance hall. Just inside, Eric removed the last of his heavy protective steel armor and dropped it with a crash on the marble floor.

The clattering alerted Curtis of Eric's presence, and he came to stand in the doorway of his small workroom opening off the main entrance hall. Eric inquired of him where he might find Lord Schmidden, and although Curtis's green eyes brimmed with curiosity, he contained himself, replying politely, "He's in the great room, sir. He's been there since you left."

Eric, highly motivated by the good news he was to deliver, moved rapidly down the corridor. He pushed open the door to the great room and then halted abruptly. There, by his massive chair which he had retrieved from the music salon, knelt Lord Schmidden, with his head in his hands. Undecided as to whether to interrupt the nobleman or quietly slip away and return later, Eric hesitated momentarily.

But Lord Schmidden had been expecting Eric. "Come in, come in, my boy!" his deep voice welcomed Eric as he rose to his feet.

Eric moved slowly into the room, trying to hide his limp. Lord Schmidden met him and gripped him in a hearty embrace. Eric had rehearsed in his mind the report he would make to Lord Schmidden, but finding him on his knees in prayer banished all thought of the battle. "Sir, I do not mean to pry," Eric swallowed hard, "but have you been there," he gestured toward the chair where Lord Schmidden had been kneeling just moments earlier, "since I left?"

"Yes, Branden. I had years of lost time to make up. I turned my back on God when Rose disappeared—but He never gave up on me!" He passed his hand over his face. "But never mind that now. Surely you have good news for me!"

"Yes, sir, I do indeed. The battle is won. God gave us victory! Your enemies are dead, and Lord Frederick's fortress is a burned-out shell."

Tears welled up in Lord Schmidden's eyes, and he exclaimed, "Words are an empty way to pay my debt to you, but I am indeed grateful. Now I can safely bring Rosamund home. Oh, thank God! Thank God!"

As the older man spoke his daughter's name, he happened to be looking Eric full in the face. He observed the change in the young man's countenance, and although Eric quickly averted his eyes, the flush that crept up his neck to suffuse his face was not lost on the older man. He raised his eyebrows, silently and suddenly keenly interested in Eric's unexpected reaction.

Eric shifted his weight, momentarily forgetting his injured leg. He grimaced at the sudden pain that shot through him, and he bent over with a groan. Blood oozed out of the awkward bandage and trickled down his leg in rivulets. Lord Schmidden instantly forgot his puzzled speculations and rang for help.

Resisting the idea that he should be treated as an invalid, Eric finally agreed to lean on Lord Schmidden. With the servants following closely behind, he limped down the corridor, through the entrance hall, and past the chapel. Then began the slow climb up the stairs toward his room in the tower. Halting every two or three steps, Eric gritted his teeth, white-faced and trembling. Now that the battle was over and a report had been made to Lord Schmidden, pain took command of his senses.

Halfway up the twenty-six steps Eric's legs buckled, and he fell heavily forward. Clutching desperately at the stone wall for a handhold, his fingers scraped down the rough surface, shaving the skin off several knuckles to expose raw, bleeding flesh. Unable to get a grip and too weak to stop himself, he lunged sideways, slamming full weight against the stone wall at the base of the step. Pain tore through his shoulder; his ear and cheek burned from the severe impact.

Before Eric's body had come to a stop, the wall made a strange grinding sound. Lord Schmidden, thrown off balance by Eric's fall, thrust out his hand toward the wall to prevent himself from falling on top of Eric. As he did so, the wall shuddered and a section of stones, about two feet wide by six feet high and two feet thick, slowly grated open. Lord Schmidden fell into the opening with a crash. He landed on his stomach with his arm—the one he'd reached out to stop his fall—extended straight out along the floor above his head, as if pointing at something.

The servants, who had been following closely behind, took one look and turned and ran, tumbling and stumbling back down the stairs. Their hysterical shrieks could be heard as far away as the scullery.

Eric groaned in pain. Lord Schmidden rolled over and sat up, his back to the opening. Slowly, gingerly, Eric straightened up on the steps and swung around to face the older man. His eyes widened in shock, first at seeing the opening in the wall and then at the eerie spectacle illuminated by the glow from the stairwell candles.

"No!" came Eric's horrified cry.

Lord Schmidden leaned forward to help Eric up, exclaiming, "Branden! I'm so sorry!" Seeing the consternation on Eric's face as he stared past the older man, Lord Schmidden thought to turn his head to see what had upset Eric.

Sensing the older man's intent, Eric's hand shot out and he clutched Lord Schmidden's knee in a desperate grip. *"Don't turn around!"* he commanded fiercely. Waves of nausea swept over Eric. The pain in his leg and hand and shoulder and face were forgotten. He put his head between his knees and sucked in air in panting gulps, trying desperately to pull himself together.

"Oh, God!" he rasped as another wave of nausea

rolled over him. Still he squeezed Lord Schmidden's knee, unconsciously, as if by sheer willful force he could somehow prevent Lord Schmidden from ever seeing the mysterious chamber's grim secret. When the nausea finally subsided, Eric raised his head. He spoke very slowly and gently, as to a child, but he never released his hold on Lord Schmidden's knee. "Lord Schmidden, in the chamber behind you, lying on the floor, there is a skeleton."

Lord Schmidden recoiled as if he'd been slapped in the face, and he leaped to his feet. He drew in his breath so loudly that Eric heard the gasp. Lord Schmidden stood immobilized. Shocked. Stricken. Horror swallowed them both.

Eric, concerned for Lord Schmidden's well-being, pulled himself upright and laid a hand on the older man's shoulder. Without speaking, together, they moved carefully toward the skeleton. In the candlelight, the diamonds in the tiara glittered and the stones in the necklace, earrings, and rings that lay in all the right places sparkled, as though tragedy had never taken place, and the remains of a satin dress shone brightly in the low light.

"It's. . ." Lord Schmidden muffled his stricken whisper as he covered his pain-distorted face with a shaking hand. He moved nearer and bent down for a closer look. "Yes, it's Rose. . .and the baby." His voice scraped, taut with emotion. "She had just told me, that evening, that we were going to have a second child!" He put out a hand and tentatively touched the sleeve of the once-beautiful party dress.

Blackness engulfed Eric, and he closed his eyes to

regain his composure, to momentarily shut out the older man's pain. His stomach resembled nothing so much as a ball of fire in his gut, and words wouldn't come. What could he say!

Surprisingly, it was Lord Schmidden who regained his composure first. He straightened up, saying, "Come, let's get you to your room. This," he waved toward the vacuous chamber, "has already waited ten years. It will keep." He grasped Eric's arm, raised it over his shoulder, and aided him, one step at a time, up to the landing outside Eric's tower room. He pushed open the door, and they hobbled in together. Both in pain.

"I think I'll soak in the bath," Eric said, beginning to strip off his soiled clothing. Then he paused, eyeing Lord Schmidden apprehensively as the older man stumbled toward the door. Would he be all right? Should he detain Lord Schmidden here where he could keep an eye on him? "Sir, what I really need is a clean bandage. There's one in my kit on the shelf," he pointed, "there, at the end."

In response to Eric's request, Lord Schmidden turned to locate the bandage. Eric carefully eased himself into the steaming water. He felt gratitude toward whoever had built up the fire and filled the bath. He stifled an exclamation as the hot water hit the open wound; it burned like fire. He gently touched the torn skin and grimaced, but he was relieved to see that he was actually missing very little skin, and the salt had prevented the infection that could have developed from the foul water in the moat. A salve dressing, a good bandage, and a few days of inactivity would put it on the mend.

Still dazed, Lord Schmidden deposited the clean

bandage on the bed and then slowly lowered himself into a nearby chair. Leaning his head on his hands, he groaned as if his heart were being torn out—a soul-wrenching cry.

Eric watched him. Silent. Everything he could think of to say sounded trite. Wisely, he said nothing and looked away out of respect and consideration.

Several minutes passed before Lord Schmidden raised his head and straightened in the chair. He began to talk aloud—to God, Eric perceived—quite as if he had forgotten Eric's presence or his own whereabouts. "No one told me about a secret chamber. I always suspected there might be one—but we couldn't find anything." Despair edged the resignation in his voice. "Rose must have fallen, running up the steps. When the wall came open she probably thought it would be a good joke to hide in there. She was a great one for pranks. I'm sure she never dreamed I wouldn't know how to get in. After all, I've lived here all my life. My great-grandfather built the place!" He bit off bitter words.

Eric wished he hadn't been trapped into listening, but he had no choice.

Still staring into space, Lord Schmidden spoke again, "Well, God, You know best. She loved You with all her heart—and I was the unfaithful one. Thank You for being so patient with my lack of trust—for being merciful. It could have been worse. Her suffering ended quickly, and now she's with You." He dropped his head into his broad hands before continuing. "Thank You for showing me what did happen to her. And the child. Now, at last, I can sleep in peace."

This expression of gratitude was shortly followed by

a low moan and another confession, as though further revelation had come to him, "Forgive me, God, for not teaching Rosamund about You! I've failed miserably. I purposely shielded her from knowing about You. I thought if You couldn't take care of Rose. . .well, I could do better than You did and Rosamund didn't need You—but I was wrong. Please, please God, forgive my foolish pride, for thinking myself wiser than You. Let me right the wrong I've done. Help me show her the way to You."

At this point, Eric, forgetting that he was listening in on another's confessions and that he had resolved to keep his feelings to himself, impulsively blurted, "But Rosamund does know God!"

Lord Schmidden's hands dropped to his knees and his neck snapped as he jerked around to look at Eric, disbelief plain on his face. His words pierced the air like daggers, "And just how would you know, Branden?"

The time had come for Eric to bare his soul, and he did so. Bravely. Haltingly. He recounted his visit with Rosamund at Edith's cottage, told of her memories of the loss of her mother, and then of finding the Book of Hours which had revealed God to her. "And sir," he stammered, "if you won't think me too bold for asking, I'd like your permission to marry her." He hesitated, then finished honestly, "You see, I love her."

The silence that followed his humble confession was so prolonged that Eric feared Lord Schmidden was considering how best to rebuke his impertinence. However, the older man finally rose to his feet, a towering figure. He turned deliberately to face Eric, "Son, you said discretion wins a war, and you certainly live by your own rules!" He shook his head, undisguised admiration on his face.

"I always wanted a son, and there's no one I'd rather give Rosamund to, no one I'd rather see take over this place. . ." His chin tightened in satisfaction. "Father my grandsons. Pray with me. Bury me. You have my whole-hearted blessing. Consider the matter arranged." And then Eric heard him whisper, more to himself than anyone, "God be praised!"

Hope had surged in Eric's heart at that first word, "son," and he struggled to control the tumult that shook him. Clearing his throat, he found his voice, "Sir, between you and me, I'm most grateful to consider the marriage arranged—but would you not tell Rosamund? Maybe it's a foolish notion, but I'd like to win her heart—if I could." Eric looked away, embarrassed to be discussing his tender affection. Lord Schmidden, on the other hand, eyed him with understanding and appreciation; God had been gracious to provide a husband for Rosamund who would share his own love for her.

On his way out the door, Lord Schmidden paused, running his long fingers through his silvery-white hair. "I'll be making the burial arrangements, and then I'll see what I can do about fetching a certain young woman!" His eyes twinkled affectionately, "And you have my word, I'll let you do the talking!"

His smile was so warm and open that Eric couldn't help grinning back. "Thank you, sir!" The appropriate words seemed so inadequate.

Lord Schmidden turned to say over his shoulder, "Let's hope *sir* will soon be *Papa!*"

That last word of acceptance erased the final vestiges

of Eric's fear, and his heart ached for his friend as he heard him going bravely down the steps to deal with the hard reality of Rose's tragic death. *God tests all men's hearts,* he thought. *One day my turn will come.*

thirteen

Early evening shadows scattered purple and blue tints like a patchwork coverlet over the castle garden. Wispy white clouds scudded across the blue sky, and the sun, dropping down to touch the mountains, was preparing to end the day's work. Rioting roses shed their fragrant magic like confetti on all who came near, and somewhere in the soft gloaming a little bird sang his evening prayer. The stone garden bench, cornered into a fragrant shadow of forest green, held a solitary visitor. Eric soaked up the last of the sun's healing rays while he observed the passing of time on the nearby sundial and drew in a deep breath of glorious evening air. Had it only been a week since the victory over Lord Frederick and the discovery of the secret chamber? Eric looked out over the beds of roses and watched a buzzing bee drift from flower to flower while he mentally reviewed the events of the past week. His crew had been divided into two units. Olaf and those men choosing to return to Sweden via Denmark had departed three days ago. Those desiring to connect with the trade route to seek sea passage back to Sweden had departed with Karl yesterday. He had assigned rights to his ship, whatever its state, to Olaf, without a single twinge of regret. God had so prepared his heart for the changes occurring in his life that the ship and the adventures it represented seemed to belong to another lifetime.

Eric's injured leg had almost completely recovered. He had discovered an amazing thing about a puncture wound: the pain is not limited to the actual site of injury; at any point along the pathway, disturbed nerves may react. In fact, his hip had caused him more discomfort than the actual wound itself. He still found himself favoring that leg, but the aching had diminished and he felt sure he would soon be as fit as ever.

Lord Schmidden had sent a messenger to the king, informing him of the outcome of this local skirmish and advising him of Eric's role in the victory. He confided to Eric his hope that a title might be bestowed on Eric in reward for his valiant heroism. The king was generous in conferring honor, however reluctant he might be to get involved in local disputes.

Lord Schmidden had also invited Eric to accompany him in riding over the newly acquired property. They would do that next week. The realization that it would all one day be his humbled the younger man. God had certainly been trustworthy. To provide him with a home and a family—and not just any family, but one with such a noble heritage—was more than he could have imagined. His heart swelled with gratitude.

And Rosamund. She would be home tomorrow! Her father had gone to bring her back, and Eric had to admit it was difficult to concentrate for long on anything else.

Pensive, he considered the plans which had been made for the interment of Rose and the baby. A casket had been prepared, but the ceremony would wait until Rosamund could be present. A priest from one of the nearby villages had been summoned to perform the service, and Eric knew Lord Schmidden planned to tell Rosamund about it before they arrived back at Burg Mosel.

The betrothal ring Lord Schmidden had given his Rose now rested in the depths of Eric's pouch, impatiently awaiting the exchange of commitment that would seal its new destiny.

The secret chamber had been thoroughly cleaned and investigated. Lord Schmidden had spoken of sealing it off, but he had decided to leave it as it was as a reminder of his renewed commitment to walk once again with God in a relationship of trust, and Eric admired Lord Schmidden for his brave decision.

In the past week the grieving man had often fallen silent, a sad expression filling his eyes, and Eric's heart ached for him. Once he tried to say something encouraging, but Lord Schmidden ended up comforting himself.

"In my rejection of God I was a lot worse off than Rose. There was so little air in that chamber I doubt she felt anything. She just went to sleep. But my spiritual death was far more slow and agonizing. Deciding to eliminate God isn't the end; it's just the beginning. Death creeps up to cut off circulation, one limb at a time. It squeezes the life out, bit by bit. Finally gangrene sets in—and bitterness is a foul-smelling pus that only God can cleanse."

He shook his leonine head. "No, son, my greatest sorrow is not Rose's death, although I've missed her terribly, missed the fulfillment of all we hoped to share, missed the child we would have had. My greatest regret is the years without the friendship of God. Life is a suffocating business without Him."

Even as Eric sat, reflecting, the sun dropped behind the distant mountains. He stood up and stretched his tall frame to full height. Still contemplative, he followed the flower-bordered cobbled walkway through the courtyard and entered the arched wooden doors that opened into the main entrance hallway. He turned to go down the corridor that led past the Chapel of the Shepherd and on to the tower stairs. As he rounded the corner, Eric halted in surprise. The heavy chain that had declared the chapel off-limits had been removed. He had frequently entertained curiosity about the sanctuary because of Rosamund's reference to sensing God's presence there, but chains had barred the doors before he'd ever arrived at Burg Mosel.

Impulse carried him through the chapel doors, and once inside, he stopped, looking around. The intricate design of the inlaid wood floor shone with a high gloss. Simple wooden kneeling pews stood at right angles along the outer walls on each side; they formed a center aisle. Arched beams embraced the walls at intervals and shouldered the graceful dome. The stained-glass Shepherd, in brilliant color, provided the room's only source of light, and He was every bit as embracing as Rosamund had implied.

The Shepherd's eyes seemed to draw him, and Eric, in response, made his way up to the altar railing and knelt. Fading daylight glowed through the window and cast an other-worldly radiance upon the face of the worshipper. When he stood to his feet, his heart felt lightened by the sense of God's presence, that same protecting Presence he had sensed looking up at the stars the first night on his journey to this place.

He turned to leave, but the burial chamber in the ante-room opening out to the left of the nave caught his attention. The ceiling was low; it obviously filled the empty space beneath the tower stairs. Inscribed in Latin on the soffit above the compartment were these words: *God is not the God of the dead, but of the living—Matthew 22:32.*

Eric moved over to the podium which stood just inside the chamber doorway. A book lay open on the stand and Eric scanned the last several entries:

> June 5, 1398 Nicklaus Schmidden and Rose
>   Glinden
> Holy Matrimony
> August 12, 1402 Leopold Schmidden. Death.
>   Plague.
> August 27, 1402 Clara Brunnell Schmidden.
>   Death. Plague.
> July 15, 1403 Rosamund Jeanne Abigail
>   Schmidden. Birth.
>   Daughter of Nicklaus and Rose Schmidden.

As he read the names and dates, it came to Eric that no final entry had ever been made for Rose Schmidden. He knew the sadness he felt could in no way compare to the talons of painful uncertainty which must have clawed at those who knew and loved her. He swallowed hard at the lump in his throat.

Abruptly, Eric closed the book and stepped up close to the stone coffins. They were stacked one upon another so only the front end of each casket was visible. There were four in each row. Some were very old, and the names etched on them could hardly be distinguished. He traced the faint markings with his finger. Elfrieda. Gunter. Lisle. Then the second row. Nicklaus. Elsa. Leopold. Clara. Beside them, again atop each other, stood smaller ones, obviously those of children. Frances. Rolf. Margaret. Anna. Heinrich. Harold. Henrietta.

Contrary to what Eric expected he would feel, he recalled again the words inscribed above the chamber. He turned and slowly made his way through the chapel, reflecting on the freedom death brings to those who know God. Resting in those burial containers were only the physical remains of people whose spirits had been released from the restraint of time to join God in eternity. There were always those who went before and those who followed after. His duty was to uphold the honor of those who had gone before him and to pass on an untarnished birthright to those who followed him.

Eric hesitated at the doors for one final look. Darkness, rather than smothering the room, served only to intensify the Shepherd. His heart surged at the promise of becoming a part of Rosamund's family: past, present, and, if God should graciously allow, future generations. He closed the chapel doors. Completely forgetting his injury, Eric took the stone stairs two at a time.

fourteen

The countryside shimmered with the sultry fragrance of summer colors, and Rosamund could hardly contain her happiness. This was the day she had waited and prayed for these long months. Papa had come for her, and they were going home!

The sadness of her mother's death and that of the unborn child had been shared with Edith, and they had wept together. Hugging them both tightly, Edith had steadied her quavering voice and whispered comforting words. "Be tellin' Rose 'hello' for ye, I will. She be waitin' for me, I mind! I be done servin' my purpose and 'spect to be soon departin' in peace."

So they had put away their grief like a keepsake, and the three of them, intuitively aware that they would never be together again on this earth, cherished each moment. They ate and laughed and listened as Lord Schmidden told of Eric's miraculous march across the frozen sea, his subsequent conquest of Lord Frederick, and of his injured leg.

Rosamund gasped when he spoke of the injury and then coughed to cover her dismay. Lord Schmidden observed his daughter's reactions, so like his own Rose, who also at times had responded from her heart instead of her head. He smiled to himself and continued speaking, relating details of the battle. Rosamund said nothing, but her silence told its own story, and Lord Schmidden had sighed in relief and satisfaction.

The next morning Rosamund woke with the birds. Restless and anxious to be going home, she dressed quickly in the least worn of Kathe's frocks. With a twinge of regret she wished for one of her own pretty dresses, nevertheless knowing that Kathe's homespun would certainly be more suitable for the long journey ahead.

Happy to be together, father and daughter rode for several hours in near silence. Three times Lord Schmidden tried to find the right words to tell Rosamund of his renewed commitment to God. But each time he tried to frame his thoughts into words, he couldn't seem to get past Eric's revelation that she had encountered God for herself. Not wanting to betray Eric's confidence, even inadvertently, he resolved to say nothing and wait, hoping his daughter would make a comment that would provide him the desired opportunity.

Rosamund, secure and content in her father's company, began to confide the details of her stay at Edith's: the amazing blizzard, the herb pouches, the fair. She deliberately left out Eric's visit but elaborated on overhearing Lord Frederick's boasting, her own fears, and the comfort she had found in the special book. His gift to her mother.

This opened the door for Lord Schmidden to express his heart. "I, too, have come back to God, Rosamund. He gave me a long leash, but He never let me go. And He's been faithful to me in spite of my failure to trust Him." Regret roughened his voice. "Forgive me for failing you, too, dear."

Rosamund saw him steady his chin, and her heart nearly burst with love and compassion. With her slender white hand, she covered her father's hand that was clenched on his knee next to hers, leaned her head on his shoulder, and whispered, "Papa, there is nothing to forgive. God has filled the emptiness in my heart and taken away the pain." He slipped his arm about her shoulders, and they rode thus, their love for each other deep and strong.

After a while, from a drowsy distance, Rosamund broke the peaceful silence, "Papa?" He didn't speak, only nodded and raised his bushy brows to indicate she had his attention. She continued. "Did we ever have a man at Burg Mosel who taught my mother to play the harpsichord?"

"Pierre—Pierre Monet." He said the name slowly, tentatively. "I haven't thought of him in years." He questioned her in surprise, "You don't remember him?" Then with a shake of his head he answered himself, "No, of course you wouldn't. He lived with us for nearly a year soon after we were married. He came back occasionally to visit after that. Why, come to think of it, he came for Josie's wedding. I guess that's the last time we ever saw him. I wonder what became of him?"

"And he taught my mother to play the harpsichord?"

"Yes." He drew his lips into a straight, disapproving line. "Quite the young stag, he was. Had all the maids swooning over him, though it seemed he had some great love in his life—he wouldn't give the girls the passing time of day. His melancholy streak was a bit much for me. I didn't relish his company. Rose knew him quite well, of course."

Lord Schmidden paused, his bushy brows descending over thoughtful eyes before he turned his head to inquire, "Why did you ask?"

Rosamund wasn't quite sure what to make of Edith's odd remark about the man in question having "made eyes" at her mother, but not wishing to rouse any question as to the reason for her curiosity, she responded to her father's question in a drowsy, disinterested tone, as though she had been half asleep, "Hmm? Oh. Edith— Edith mentioned him." She would think about it all later.

With a lazy stretch she sat up, deliberately ending the subject by moving the conversation on in a brighter vein. "Papa, is Eric's crew still at Burg Mosel?" It was an indirect way to ask about Eric, but she couldn't quite bring herself to ask straight out.

"No. They're gone. They separated into two groups and left several days ago. They hope to get back to Sweden before bad weather sets in."

Rosamund's heart sank. What else was there to say? Eric had gone. She was silent the rest of the journey home.

When Burg Mosel came into view, proud and grand with its bright blue banner waving a welcome to them in the late afternoon sunshine, Rosamund became restless. She had missed her home. And Kathe. And Pfeiffer.

When the carriage crossed the long cobbled drive, she clutched at her father's sleeve, her face flushed and her eyes sparkling with excitement. She stood up almost before they had come to a stop; she was out of the carriage and fairly flying up the long flight of steps. She flashed through the front doors like a streak of lightning.

Rushing through the main entrance hallway, she nodded to her ancestors on either side as she whizzed by. She laughed softly to herself. Funny, they didn't seem at all like the glowering faces she had left behind!

Dashing down the back stairs toward the scullery, Rosamund let her fingers once again vibrate over the rough stones, but this time her thoughts tingled with anticipation. Soon she would see Kathe!

In her haste she tripped at the bottom step. Her feet slid out from under her. With a rude thud she bumped to an inglorious stop on the cold stones. Stunned, she sat there for a minute to collect her scattered dignity. "Rosamund, sometimes you're so impulsive. When will you act like a lady?" she laughingly admonished herself under her breath, undaunted by the spill.

Then her mouth dropped open in dismay. It couldn't be happening again! But it was. Her ears burned at the conversation taking place in the scullery, which she couldn't help overhearing: "I wonder how Miss Rosamund will like finding herself the prize for winning her papa's war?"

Rosamund's head jerked up, her eyes narrowed, and a frown froze her face. Herself the prize! Whose prize? Who was that, gossiping, anyway? It sounded like Letty.

Then she heard Hildy's familiar voice, "Now, Letty, how came you by this notion?"

So it *was* Letty. She never had trusted the cook!

Rosamund could almost hear Letty's smirk. "Matilda and I went back up the stairs after Lord Schmidden and Master Eric found Lady Rose in that there chamber. They were in the tower room, and they left the door open a crack, and I heard Lord Schmidden tellin' Master Eric that the marriage was set." She hardly took a breath. "I'd have heard more, too, but Matilda pulled me away 'cause she was afraid we'd be caught." Rosamund heard a loud bang as if Letty had slammed down a kettle to emphasize her statement. "There now, d'you doubt my word?"

Rosamund leaped to her feet. Angry. Humiliated. Without stopping to think, she burst through the doorway, her blue eyes throwing sparks. Heads jerked. Guilty faces blanched. Several astonished maids dropped what they were doing. A kettle splashed into a pan full of water. A crockery bowl smashed to bits on the stone floor.

Pairs of horrified eyes riveted on Lord Schmidden's daughter. Rosamund! Here! Of course the servants talked about the nobility they served—but it was considered shameful to ever be caught. And Rosamund had heard their indiscretion; there could be no doubt!

"For shame! I shall speak to Papa about this! Clean up that mess," she pointed an accusing finger at the shattered shard, "and see to it you mind your own business!" Her angry words scorched. She turned and fled back up the stairs and out the back door. Indignation burned up her tears. What a welcome!

Rosamund rushed along the hedge and across the stable yard. She pushed open the door to the stable. She passed the long row of stalls and the empty pens. Forgetting her dress and ignoring the gate, she flung herself over the bars into Pfeiffer's pen and wrapped her arms around the horse's neck. He turned his head toward her, nickering a welcome. "Dear old Pfeiffer. You're a faithful friend!" she whispered brokenly.

Waves of confusing emotion flooded over her.

Betrayal! How *could* Papa arrange a marriage for her without even *asking* her?

Anger! How *could* Eric agree to marry her without knowing if she *liked* him—much less loved him? Her dreams lay shattered like the shard. Broken into pieces.

Insult! How *could* Letty repeat such gossip to the servants in the scullery?

Frustration! Why did it *hurt* so badly to think Eric and Papa had disposed of her future in such a cold manner?

Shock! She *loved* Eric! That's why it hurt! A moan escaped her lips. The truth hit her with such force that the stiffening went out of her legs. She loved someone who could coldly decide she would be an adequate reward! First Lord Frederick's villainous betrayal, and now this! Oh, the shame of it!

Heartsick, she sank into the straw, shaking with wild sobbing and hot tears. She grabbed at the straw, flicking it into the air in angry jerks. Her cheeks burned and the laces down the back of Kathe's old dress seemed much too tight. She could hardly breathe.

Pfeiffer, only knowing that his mistress was behaving strangely, nuzzled up to her. She calmed a bit and raised herself into a sitting position. She wiped her eyes on her sleeve, still sniffling and hiccuping.

A familiar deep voice spoke softly from somewhere near the railing, "Rosamund, whatever is the matter? Is there anything I can do to help you?"

Rosamund's teary eyes popped open, and she was on her feet in an instant. Eric! What was he doing here? How long had he been standing there? Fury mingled with embarrassment. "You! How could you?" she burst out. Casting about, revenge swelling up within her, eyes burning blue, she grabbed the nearest object. A bucket. Thinking to fling its liquid contents on Eric, she heaved it at him. She knew in an instant that later she would regret losing her dignity, but for the moment it was intensely satisfying.

Horror threatened to overcome her; it wasn't water! The air mushroomed with a gray cloud of Pfeiffer's feed. And worse, Eric dodged! She gagged on the feed dust, coughing and choking uncontrollably. Scratchy particles caught in her nose and throat. Tears ran down her face. Was he laughing at her?

She glared at him angrily. Glared at the empty bucket she still clutched. Glared again at an astounded, wide-eyed Eric. Infuriated at her failure to execute revenge, she gritted her teeth and ground out an exclamation of exasperation. "Rrrrr."

Disconcerted, Eric stared at her. But his speechlessness only magnified her mortification. Flustered and enraged, she pitched the empty bucket into the corner, jerked open the gate to Pfeiffer's pen, and stormed, still fuming, out of the stable. She ran across the stable yard and along the length of the hedge toward the back doors. Her eyes stung with tears—whether of anger, shame, humiliation, or disappointment, she didn't quite know. And all the while she muttered threats of vengeance beneath her breath. She twitched her skirt roughly when it caught on something, she didn't bother to see what, and she yanked it free, almost relishing the ripping that followed.

She clutched her torn skirt with both hands and ran up the stairs and down the long corridor to her own room.

With a vicious thrust she slammed the door behind her and flung herself on her bed. Sobbing, she pounded the coverlet with her fist in frustration. At last a disconsolate Rosamund crumpled forlornly in the middle of the bed.

Gradually, the gentle peace and familiarity of her own room massaged her hurt pride like a balm, and she began to relax. Everything was just as she had left it. The blue-and-white bed curtains, tied back with cords and tassels, were fresh and crisp as a spring sky. The leaded-glass window smiled light into the pretty room. The coramandel screen with its vines and flowers, imported from the East, divided the long room into a sleeping space and a cozy sitting area. The fireplace hinted of warmth, and dark paneling made a delightful backdrop for the settee with its polished wood and blue brocade cushions, the dainty dressing table and curved-back chair, the navy-and-cream hand-tied wool rug, the massive silver sticks holding candles for illuminating the night. Home!

Leaning up on one elbow, her eyes fell on the trunk and chest that had been carried up for her by the servants. With a sudden urgency, she slid off the bed and began to open the small chest with frantic fingers. When she finally held the book in her hands, she clasped it tightly to her chest and sat on the edge of the bed. The words of this book had given her comfort before. Maybe God could help her think clearly about her new trouble.

She laid the book face down on the bed, undid the clasp, and opened it from the back. She didn't want to see that yellow rose today! And she didn't want to consider why she felt that way, either! Using her thumb, she flipped the pages and stopped at Hour Fourteen.

Bow down thine ear,
O Lord, hear me: for I am poor and needy.
Preserve my soul; for I am holy:
O thou my God, save thy servant that
trusteth in thee.
Be merciful unto me, O Lord: for I cry unto
thee daily.
Rejoice the soul of thy servant: for unto thee,
O Lord, do I lift up my soul.
For thou, Lord, art good, and ready to forgive;
And plenteous in mercy unto all them that
call upon thee.
Give ear, O Lord, unto my prayer;
And attend to the voice of my supplications.
In the day of my trouble I will call upon thee:
For thou wilt answer me.
Teach me thy way, O Lord;
I will walk in thy truth:
Unite my heart to fear thy name.
I will praise thee, O Lord my God, with all
my heart:
And I will glorify thy name forevermore.
For great is thy mercy toward me:
And thou hast delivered my soul from the
lowest hell.
O God, the proud are risen against me,
And the assemblies of violent men have
sought after my soul;
And have not set thee before them.
But thou, O Lord, art a God full of compassion,
and gracious,
Longsuffering, and plenteous in mercy and truth.

> O turn unto me and have mercy upon me;
> Give thy strength unto thy servant,
>   And save the son of thine handmaid.
> Show me a token for good;
>   That they which hate me may see it, and be
>   ashamed:
> Because thou, Lord, hast helped me, and com-
>   forted me.
> —Psalm 86

As if her own heart had written them, she whispered the words out loud: "Save me, Your servant who trusts in You. . . Bring joy to the heart of me, Your servant. . . I am so glad that You are forgiving and good. . . Be my Teacher so I will walk in Your truth. . . Give me a sign of Your goodness. . . Because of Your love, I am helped and comforted."

She closed the volume, refastened the clasp. Hugging the book to her heart, she lay back on the bed. Her anger dissipated. It really didn't matter what Papa and Eric had done. She was only responsible for herself. And she knew she was wrong on two counts. She had assumed Letty's gossip was true, and she had lost her temper and behaved shamefully.

She swallowed hard at the thought of apologizing. However, not one to remain idle once a decision had been made, she jumped up and began scurrying about the room. No time for a maid today! She ripped off the ugly, torn dress, leaving it where it fell. With hasty jerks she pulled on one of her own, the soft blue silk. Oh, yes! And the wide lace collar. She cinched in the waist and fastened her mother's pearl earrings on her ears.

Without thinking, she scuffed off the heavy shoes and then hopped about on the cold floor until she located fresh stockings and a pair of soft leather slippers.

She brushed her disheveled hair vigorously and was amazed at the wisps of straw that floated to the floor. She must have looked like a barnyard fowl when she had flown at Eric! She burned with shame and brushed even harder.

When she had twisted her hair up and back, fastening it in a mature, sophisticated style—most unlike her recent behavior—she said aloud to herself, "If I must eat humble pie, perhaps looking pretty will help it taste better!"

With water from the pitcher on the bedside table, she rinsed her face and hands and dried them on the cotton towel with dainty flowers stitched on one edge that lay waiting for her use.

Catching up a feather plume from her dressing table, she twitched it nervously to cool her cheeks. A determined look came over her face. She would go have a talk with Papa.

fifteen

The situation appeared quite different from Eric's perspective. He had been visiting with Curtis in his small front workroom when Rosamund flashed into the castle and darted for the stairs. With great effort he continued speaking with Curtis. He didn't wish to be rude—or to reveal the sudden pounding in his chest—but he ended the conversation as hastily as he politely could and turned to leave. He heard echoing footsteps coming up the scullery stairs, and he stopped in the doorway. He saw Rosamund rush for the back door, then heard the thud as it banged shut behind her.

Eric followed her, stepping outside just in time to see her disappear into the stables. He crossed the stable yard and pushed open the heavy door. Quietly, he slipped inside. Rosamund's hysterical sobs arrested him. Whatever could be wrong? She had always seemed so self-contained.

He followed her sobs until he stood outside Pfeiffer's pen, arriving just in time to see her sink to the straw in a heap of distress. Girls and their tears were not always easy for Eric to understand, and even with a younger sister and five sisters-in-law, he felt helpless. Perplexed. He leaned on the rails and waited, casting about in his mind for something to say.

When her weep-fest subsided, Rosamund sat up.

Dabbing at her tearstained face, she left streaks and smudges on cheeks and chin. Her dark hair was frosted with a golden halo of straw, and despite her distress, she looked to Eric like an angel. Unaware he played a role in her anguish, he gently offered to help, "Rosamund, whatever is the matter? Is there anything I can do to help you?"

Her violent reaction, however, shocked him speechless. His mouth dropped open when she leaped to her feet, sending straw flying everywhere, and struck out at him like an angry rooster. "You! How could you?"

Eric saw her reach down for the nearby bucket. Reading malicious intent in her eyes, he sidestepped the oncoming cloud of feed dust. He squinted at her through it and saw her glare at him in his unscathed condition. She eyed the now empty feed bucket and then looked back to him. He perceived her chagrin at her backfired efforts, but he remained paralyzed, stunned by her shocking behavior. What had become of the girl of his dreams?

Vexed, she stomped her foot, emitting angry noises. She jerked open the gate to Pfeiffer's pen and fled out of the stable.

Eric rubbed a hand over his face as if he had been clawed. Betraying his shock by movements that were more automatic than deliberate, he closed his still gaping mouth and closed the swinging gate to Pfeiffer's pen. Puzzled, considering, he stood staring at the empty straw. He closed his eyes and shook his head as if to clear his mind. Then resolve turned him on his heel, and he followed Rosamund out of the stable.

Eric found Lord Schmidden in the entrance hallway,

talking to Curtis. He interrupted them awkwardly, his voice strained, "Sir, I need to speak to you at once. I'll be waiting in the great room." He turned abruptly, not waiting for Lord Schmidden to respond.

Lord Schmidden turned to eye Eric's retreating figure, puzzled by his unusual behavior. Looking back to his curious-eyed clerk, he excused himself. "I'll talk to you later, Curtis." Quickly, the older man followed Eric along the corridor and into the great room.

All signs of military engagement had been removed from the large hall, and the room reflected its former elegance. The two heavy chairs and the little stool were once again in their familiar positions by the fire. Lord Schmidden motioned the distraught Eric to be seated, and he sat down in his favorite chair. One bushy eyebrow quirked up as he inquired, "Now then, what's on your mind, Branden?"

Eric, not normally finding speech difficult, stammered and stumbled over his words while Lord Schmidden regarded him in keen surprise. "Well, sir," Eric scratched his head, "I don't rightly know." Nearly incoherent, Eric cleared his throat and began again. "At least, I mean, why is she so angry? What is it I'm supposed to have done?" He threw out his hands in confused desperation.

Lord Schmidden had to think a minute before he understood Eric's strange questions. Although he managed not to smile, his blue eyes under their bushy brows twinkled with amusement. Eric Branden could lead an army to victory, but in matters of the heart he couldn't see for the fog!

"Assuming *her* is Rosamund, what did you say to her?" he probed patiently.

A look of frustration crossed Eric's face. "That's just it! I don't know!"

"What do you mean, you don't know?"

"Well, sir, when I saw how upset—"

"Upset?" Lord Schmidden interrupted sharply.

"Why, yes—so I offered to help her."

"And what did you offer to help her with?" Lord Schmidden pinched his lower lip reflectively with thumb and forefinger.

"That's the problem! I don't know."

Lord Schmidden struggled to hold back a chuckle at Eric's frustration. "Let's back up. Where did you first see Rosamund?"

In sheer desperation Eric enunciated each syllable slowly and clearly. "She came into the entrance hall and headed down the scullery stairs."

"Did you follow her?"

"No, not then."

"All right. Then what happened?"

"In a few minutes she came running back up the stairs. She rushed out the back and banged the door."

"Hmmm. And where were you?"

"Speaking with Curtis, sir. In his office."

"And then?"

"I excused myself and followed Rosamund."

"Where did she go?"

"To the stables, sir."

"Did you go after her?"

"Yes—but she didn't see me."

"Oh. And why is that? Didn't you want her to see you?"

"No, sir. At least, that is, not right away."

Lord Schmidden drew down his heavy brows and growled, "And why not?"

"Well, because she was crying in the horse pen."

Gripping the arms of his chair and halfway rising out of it, Lord Schmidden exclaimed, "Crying in the horse pen!" He sank back in dismay. His fingers felt stiff, permanently fixed around the arms of his wooden chair.

Eric sighed. "Yes, sir. So I asked her what was troubling her, and I offered to help her."

Lord Schmidden relaxed his grip on the chair and stretched out his fingers. "And?" Eyes on his hands, he repeated the finger-stretching several more times.

"Well, she seemed shocked to see me, sir. Didn't she know I was still here?" His blue eyes bored into the eyes of the older gentleman.

Lord Schmidden was thoughtful for a moment. "Come to think of it, I guess I didn't tell her." He took a deep breath and remarked in a puzzled voice, "But that shouldn't have upset her enough to make her cry. I got the impression she likes you."

"Well, I doubt it! She threw a bucketful of feed at me!"

"She *what?*" Lord Schmidden barked. Visibly struggling to get himself under control, he leaned his elbows on the chair arms and pressed the tips of his fingers together. He frowned, concentrating. "Didn't she *say* anything?"

Eric, by now exasperated, shot back, "She said something like, 'How could you?' She was terribly upset, sir. And I was so shocked!"

"And what is it she thinks you've done?"

"That's just it! I don't know, sir! She ran out of the

stable." He stopped short, adding as an afterthought, "I didn't know what to think—so I came to you." Then almost under his breath, as though talking to himself, he added with a groan, "She's so beautiful, even when she's angry." He passed a shaking hand over his eyes.

In spite of his concern, Lord Schmidden had to stifle another chuckle before he suggested, "Well, my boy, the best thing you can do is talk to Rosamund herself."

"I don't want to talk to her. She has a beastly temper!" Eric retorted, struggling with disillusionment; his angel was flesh and blood.

Lord Schmidden rose to his feet, agreeing, "You're right! I'll talk to her. Now, you just lean back and relax for a few minutes. We'll get this all straightened out in no time." His tone was both conciliatory and indulgent. He moved to the sideboard where he poured them each a soothing drink.

The two men sat in silence; Eric desperately telling himself everything would work out and Lord Schmidden trying to stifle his inopportune mirth. Life would never be dull for these two if today held any portent of the future!

Lord Schmidden had almost resolved to go looking for his daughter when he heard her soft footfalls in the hall. The steps came closer, and in a moment she moved into the room, as beautiful and gracious as Esther, the queen.

Lost in his own thoughts, his head leaning on his hand and his eyes closed, Eric missed seeing Rosamund enter. But she saw him! She stopped dead, and then fluttered as if she were a bird about to take flight.

Lord Schmidden rose to his feet and spoke quickly to

forestall further conflict, "Come in, Rosamund, dear. It seems you and I need to have a talk." He turned to Eric, who by now had his eyes open and was staring, transfixed. "Would you please excuse us, Branden? Why don't you wait for us in the garden?"

Eric rose to leave, his eyes still fastened on Rosamund. She, on the other hand, felt disconcerted and quite unable to hold his blue glance. It was too penetrating. With relief, she watched him leave.

As soon as Eric was out of earshot, Rosamund started to protest. She wasn't sure she wanted to join Eric later—in the garden or, for that matter, anywhere at all. But again Lord Schmidden spoke first. "Come here, dear." He caught her hand and drew her onto his knee. "Now, why don't you tell your Papa all about it?" he invited in a disarming voice.

She drew in a ragged breath and asked, "Papa, how could you?"

Lord Schmidden shook his head, and if he hadn't thought he might further damage poor Rosamund's obviously already injured feelings, he would have laughed out loud. But instead he gently turned her chin so she had to look into his eyes. "How could I do what, Rosamund?"

The pitch of her voice went up several degrees and tears lurked just out of sight. "Why, Papa, how could you promise to give me to Eric as a reward for winning your stupid war?"

What had been so important was now irrelevant! Lord Schmidden smothered his smile. Rosamund clutched desperately at what few shreds of dignity she had left as she swallowed hard. Lord Schmidden soothed her with a tender voice and gently patted her shoulder. "My dear, my dear. Is that what this is all about?" He eyed her shrewdly. "Don't you like Eric?"

"Why, yes, but—" She stopped abruptly, biting her lip. Her face flushed at her untoward admission.

"But what, my dear?" *Aha! Now I'm getting somewhere,* he thought.

"Well, I want him to like me for me, and not because . . ." Too embarrassed to finish, she buried her maidenly blush against Papa's shoulder.

Lord Schmidden patted her back and smoothed her hair away from her forehead. He whispered softly. "Rosamund, Rosamund. Offering you as a reward for winning the war was never part of our discussion." His arms tightened. "Eric loves you, and I gave him permission to ask you to marry him."

Rosamund's hunched figure tensed. Then she bounced up and leaned away from him so hastily that she nearly slipped from her perch on his knee. Her dewy eyes were spangled with hope like a rainbow after a shower. "Really, Papa? Did you—does he *really?*" Could it be true? Oh, how she wanted to believe him!

"I think that's something he hopes to tell you himself," Lord Schmidden evaded with an indulgent smile.

She jumped to her feet, exclaiming, "I must go apologize. I treated him so shamefully, Papa!"

An elfish look of chagrin, pride, and mischief mingled across her face as Lord Schmidden nodded, saying dryly, "I know all about it!"

Not halfway to the door, she stopped. Hesitated. Looked back. She twitched the feather plume in her restless fingers. "You don't think he'll have changed his mind? I did behave dreadfully, Papa." Anxiety was written on her face.

Lord Schmidden's eyes twinkled merrily, and he disciplined the smile that tugged once again at the corners of his mouth as he reassured her, "No, my dear, I'm sure he won't."

She ran back to him, pulled down his noble head for a quick kiss, and then disappeared out the door.

Lord Schmidden headed for the stairs. His shoulders shook with mirth. He hadn't had such a good laugh in a long time.

sixteen

Completely forgetting her earlier intentions to be dignified, Rosamund hurried toward the castle garden. Not seeing Eric at once, she stopped in sudden panic. Where was he? Maybe Papa was wrong after all! Oh, he couldn't be! He just couldn't be! Please, God!

Her heart jumped into her throat when she spotted him. He had his back to her, frustration written in every line of his body. He was pacing back and forth in front of the stone bench. His hands gripped the hem of his tabard, and the cords in his neck stood out, reflecting the tension that tied up his insides. Preoccupied, he didn't hear her approach.

Rosamund paused, suddenly shy, a few feet away from him. Summoning all her courage, she softly called his name. "Eric."

He stopped dead, pinioned by darts of fear, anxiety, passion, pain that struck him from every side.

Fear spiraled through Rosamund's mind, but she smothered her apprehensions and valiantly refused to give in to the desire to run away as fast and as far as possible. "Eric." Bravely she whispered his name again. This time her voice carried question and apology.

He turned slowly, eyeing her with a mixture of hurt and hope, and she dropped her head, eyes on her slender fingers, fingers that had become very busy smoothing the feather plume. She bit her lips to control their quiver. Her long lashes brushed her white cheeks. Tormented. Tormenting.

"What is it you think I've done?" Eric's throbbing, anguished words defined the space between them.

Rosamund's heart tripped up her voice, which came out in a meek little sliver. "I overheard Letty say—" she gave the feather plume a diffident twitch— "that I was to be your prize for winning Papa's war." Her eyes remained downcast, and her chin was as far down as it could go. Scarlet mortification spread to the widow's peak framing her face. She poked at the cobblestones in the walkway with the toe of her leather slipper.

Eric was silent so long that Rosamund ever-so-slowly opened her eyes to peek up at him. She saw startled comprehension reflected on his face. The look of a hurt little boy lurked in his eyes as he said slowly, each word a painful thing, "I'm sorry you would have minded if that were true."

Eric's obvious misunderstanding snapped the bands of fear that had squeezed her heart. She moved close to him, clasped his arm with slender fingers, and looked up earnestly into his burning blue eyes. Sensing the damage she had done, she protested, "But I wouldn't have minded at all!"

Not understanding what she meant, Eric heard her words as so much double-talk. Tried beyond endurance, he jerked free from her grasp. "Don't tease me, Rosamund!" He turned away to hide his pain. "I don't want your pity!" He began to walk away from her. His shoulders were slumped, and disillusionment hung about him like a cloak.

"But I do love you!" she announced desperately. "I came here to apologize for losing my temper and behaving badly."

His back was a wall of steel.

She tried again, "Papa said you'd forgive me. Oh, please, you will, won't you?" She swallowed a frantic cry. *Oh, God, help me control my tongue from this day forward!*

Eric hesitated, then stopped. Rosamund held her breath. Slowly, almost fearfully, he turned to face her. "Do you know what you're saying?" His words could have impaled her with their piercing intensity.

With all the confidence she possessed, sure now of his love, Rosamund answered boldly, "Yes, I do." She smiled up at him, "I love you, Eric Branden."

He took a step toward her. "Rosamund!"

She went straight into his waiting arms, and he held her as if he would never let her go. He pressed tender kisses on her shining crown of hair, her dewy eyes, the tip of her perfect little nose, the dimple in her cheek, the hollow of her throat. And then his mouth found hers. He kissed her, gently at first and then with pent-up longing that demanded a response. She lifted her hands to caress his face and lost her fingers in his hair.

And from a window up above Lord Schmidden looked down. He smiled and nodded—to himself and to God. His Rosamund was where she belonged.

&

The lovers spent a tranquil hour in the castle garden, serenaded by the busy bees. The setting summer sun beamed down on them, and the cloudless sky stretched out across forever, its red and purple and gold pronouncing an iridescent blessing on the happy pair. But Eric and Rosamund didn't notice. They were lost in the wonder of loving and being loved.

Demurely, Rosamund voiced the age-old question asked by every lover, "When did you know that you loved me?"

Eric's eyes darkened as he recalled that poignant moment when he first realized little Rosamund had become a beautiful woman. "You smiled up at me in the firelight of Edith's cottage, and I knew why no girl had ever interested me. You were in my heart—had been for years." He silenced her attempt to speak with a kiss, as if to prove the truth of his confession.

Following a tender interlude, he repeated her query. Rosamund raised clear, shining eyes to his. "I loved you, too. All along. But I didn't know it until I overheard Letty say I was to be your prize for winning Papa's war. I had hoped you would want me for myself. Thinking you and Papa had so coldly made a business arrangement over me hurt unbearably. That's why I was crying in the stable—"

"And threw the bucketful of feed at me!" he interrupted, clasping her close in his arms and chuckling against her hair.

She drew back, her pink cheeks revealing sweet chagrin. "Oh, Eric, I *am* so sorry for the way I treated you."

His arms tightened. "Well, I'm not! What a wonderful story to tell our children! Besides, now I'm *sure* you love me!" The look in his eyes erased her embarrassment, and they laughed together the way lovers do over secrets shared.

Eric picked a rose from a nearby bush and raised it to smell its sweet perfume. "A rose for my Rose," he whispered, slipping it into the shining dark hair above Rosamund's ear. It was a yellow rose.

She relaxed in the circle of his arms. Her dimpled, smiling cheek rested against his chest. His steady heartbeat filled her with happiness. In her contentment she murmured, "Did you know that after you visited us at Feste Burg, I could hardly wait each spring to go back? I climbed the tower stairs every morning to look for you—yes, I did!" she protested when he held her away in surprise. "For five years, I did!"

"You darling!" he exclaimed. He hugged her close and then burst out, "Just think, if Lord Frederick hadn't threatened your father, I'd never have come back. God moved heaven and earth to bring us together."

After a tender moment he bent to question in her ear, "Now that I've come back, how soon will you marry me?"

A serious look crossed her face as she raised suddenly shadowed eyes to his. "Papa has arranged for a priest to come on Sunday afternoon to speak the service for Mama and the baby. If it wouldn't be too painful for Papa, we could be married the same day." Her eyes cleared with hope, "Shall we go ask him?" Her bright anticipation filled Eric's heart with such a burst of joy that he had to catch his breath.

Hand in hand they crossed the courtyard, entered the arched doors, and crossed the entrance hall. Simultaneously they saw that the chapel doors stood ajar. Exchanging an apprehensive glance—the chapel could prove to be a very emotional place for Rosamund's father—they paused in the doorway.

Lord Schmidden had been on his way out of the chapel. When he saw them enter, hands clasped together and faces shining, he hurried toward them. His happy words reached them first. "I see you both finally got your heads going in the same direction!" His chuckle warmed their hearts, and he hugged them both, one in each arm, when he met them. "So when is the wedding?" he inquired, relaxing his embrace.

Concern filled Rosamund's eyes. "That's what we were coming to talk with you about, Papa." Worry puckered her smooth forehead. "The priest will be here on Sunday to say Mama's service. Would it be all right if we had him say the marriage vows following the service?"

The muscles around Lord Schmidden's mouth tightened momentarily, and a faraway look filled his eyes. He looked up toward the stained-glass Shepherd in the chapel window and whispered brokenly, "It would be the very happy ending to so many long years of pain." He turned abruptly and walked out.

Eric and Rosamund let him go, compassion drawing them into a silent embrace. There are times when love makes words unnecessary.

seventeen

"Amen and amen." The priest pronounced the final words of the funeral service for Lady Rose Schmidden. Lord Schmidden, Rosamund, and Eric Branden raised their bowed heads, wiped away their silent tears, and rose to their feet from the kneeling benches in the Chapel of the Shepherd. Without speaking, they stepped into the aisle and moved toward the burial nave.

Lord Schmidden paused by the podium. Rosamund and Eric came up behind him and listened while he read aloud the recent entry:

> May 21, 1412 Rose Marie Glinden Schmidden
>   and infant.
> Death, suffocation. Interment August 18, 1423.

Lord Schmidden took a deep breath and cleared his throat. Rosamund reached out to smooth his shoulder sympathetically. He read the words of the final entry as he followed along with a broad pointing finger:

> August 18, 1423 Rosamund Jeanne Abigail
>   Schmidden and Eric Branden.
> Holy Matrimony.

He set aside his own grief and turned to smile at the

young couple. "Well, what are we waiting for?"

Eric, in a fresh white shirt and embroidered blue tabard that topped his well-fitting hose and matched the blue of his eyes, caught Rosamund's hand and squeezed it. Wearing the trailing ivory silk dress that had been her mother's, which Matilda had delightedly produced from the wardrobe in what had been Lady Rose's suite, Rosamund was the picture of happiness. The tucked bodice fit perfectly, and the softly gathered skirt fell from a low waist that dipped to a point in the center front. Her rosy cheeks and starry eyes were a joy to behold.

The smiling couple moved to take their places before the altar while Lord Schmidden spoke to Curtis, who had been waiting outside the closed chapel doors during the funeral service. "Ring the bell so everyone can join us," he instructed.

Presently the chapel pews began to fill with the household servants, hushed in awe. Each one had waited anxiously to see the happy bride, their own dear Rosamund.

While the servants were assembling, Eric's eyes drifted to the Shepherd in the glass—but his thoughts raced back over the events of yesterday. Following a quiet dinner, Eric and Rosamund had joined Lord Schmidden in the great room.

"Would you play for us?" Lord Schmidden had requested of his daughter, whereupon she had parted the curtains partitioning off the music salon and swagged them into brass hooks on either side of the broad doorway. Eric lit the candles in the candle stand that stood a short distance behind the harpsichord bench, and Rosamund slipped into her familiar place. Lord Schmidden eased himself into his favorite chair, leaned back his head, and closed his eyes. Peace had come to his household. God had been faithful!

The ambiance of sweet music and softly glowing candlelight enhanced the beauty of the evening. Eric leaned one elbow on the lid of the harpsichord and lost himself in admiring the lovely girl who would the next day become his wife. Her charm and grace had so captivated his thoughts that he'd taken little note when Matilda entered the great room and spoke quietly to Lord Schmidden, who responded with a nod and a smile.

Matilda disappeared through the doorway, and Lord Schmidden rose and moved toward the music salon. His approach snapped Eric from his reverie; he straightened up, a question in his eyes. Rosamund glanced up at Eric when he shifted his position, and she followed his eyes with hers. They watched her father as he entered the room. Rosamund quickly resolved the chords and ended the music.

Lord Schmidden addressed them, excitement roughening his voice. "A representative is here from the king. He's come because of the message I sent to report Eric's head-and-shoulders victory over Lord Frederick." He looked directly at Eric, "I hope he honors you well, my boy."

Eric's heart had leaped, not just at the prospective honor awaiting him, but at the hearty affection in the older man's voice and the adoration and pride on the face of the lovely girl who clasped his arm in a quick squeeze of excitement.

The three of them moved into the great room. Shortly, footsteps echoed in the corridor, coming closer, loud and heavy-heeled. And then Matilda preceded an official-looking gentleman into the great room. Lord Schmidden, Eric, and Rosamund stood at attention as the court official approached. Matilda presented the gentleman in her most formal voice, "Sir Roland to see you, Lord Schmidden."

Sir Roland bowed politely, and Lord Schmidden returned the greeting. "Welcome, sir, and a good day to you." He gestured to the young pair standing close to him, "My daughter, Rosamund, and soon-to-be son-in-law, Eric Branden."

Sir Roland nodded his acknowledgment. Then, obviously a man given to efficiency, he stated his errand in clipped tones. "In response to your message to the king, he has dispatched me to bestow upon Eric Branden the honor of an invitation to serve as a knight in the Order of Christ, upon his consent to uphold the vows of the Order."

"And what might those be, sir?" Eric inquired.

Sir Roland then proceeded to repeat the charge. "I vow to protect the Church. I vow to fight against treachery. I vow to reverence the priesthood. I vow to fend off injustice from the poor. I vow to make peace in my province. I vow to lay down my life to fulfill these commitments."

Eric agreed to uphold the commitment, and Sir Roland instructed him to kneel. Drawing his sword from its sheath, he ceremonially tapped Eric on the shoulders, first on the right and then on the left. He recited the ritual, "I, Sir Roland, by the authority invested in me by the king, do hereby dub you Sir Eric Branden, Knight Commander of the Order of Christ. Rise and serve in the name of God and your king."

Eric stood, tall and strong. And the suspiciously bright eyes of Matilda, Rosamund, and Lord Schmidden reflected their pride and gratitude.

Sir Roland produced a rolled parchment; he broke the seal and with a flourish unrolled the document. It was inscribed with a detailed coat of arms: the heraldic charge—a regardant dear, the crest, mantle, and motto in red, the helm in sable, and crowned and gorged in silver with a gold escutcheon from which was suspended an annulet engraved with a crown and Eric Branden's initials. Sir Roland read aloud the motto identifying Eric's heroism: "He who has captured a fortress and burned it."

Suddenly the pressure of Rosamund's hand on his arm brought Eric back from his memories to the reality of this moment in time that would seal the fulfillment of his dreams, the answer to his prayers. A wife. A home. A place to belong.

What a brave man, my papa! Rosamund thought, observing her father's proud carriage and noble bearing while he spoke quietly with the priest. His smile came readily, and once she even heard his low chuckle. *Oh, thank You, God, for Your healing power!*

Hildy and Kathe, their faces beaming with pride, entered the chapel. Rosamund smiled at them, relieved to be back on intimate terms with these dear folk. She had apologized for her outburst of temper, and each of the scullery maids had sought her out to make right their participation in Letty's gossip. Letty herself had quite humbly apologized for her talebearing tongue, and

Rosamund pardoned her, hoping the lesson would prove well-taken. She continued to gaze around the room; she nodded and smiled at each one whose glance met hers. Her joy was full; her cup was running over.

She looked up at the handsome man standing motionless beside her with his blue eyes fixed on the stained-glass Shepherd. He appeared lost in thought. Gently she laid her hand on his arm, calling his attention to the present moment. Eric turned his head to look at her, and their eyes met in a look of tenderness and affection that touched the hearts of all who witnessed it.

The bridal couple turned to face the altar. A hush fell over the guests. "With this ring I thee wed. . ." The words of the ancient matrimonial vows were intoned faithfully.

Eric placed on his bride's finger the ring that had been her mother's. "I now pronounce you *husband and wife.* What God has joined together, let not man put asunder." The words rang out and Eric kissed his bride.

At that instant, in the midst of their joy, a brilliant ray of sunlight burst through the stained-glass Shepherd. It spotlighted the young couple, illuminating them in a fiery halo of jeweled color. It was as if the Holy Spirit had set His seal of approval on their union. An audible gasp echoed through the sanctuary; those present were awestruck by the tangible sign of heaven's pleasure: a holy benediction complete with God's "Amen."

A Letter To Our Readers

Dear Reader:

In order that we might better contribute to your reading enjoyment, we would appreciate your taking a few minutes to respond to the following questions. When completed, please return to the following:

Rebecca Germany, Managing Editor
Heartsong Presents
P.O. Box 719
Uhrichsville, Ohio 44683

1. Did you enjoy reading *The Lady Rose?*
   - ❑ Very much. I would like to see more books by this author!
   - ❑ Moderately
     I would have enjoyed it more if _____

     _____

2. Are you a member of **Heartsong Presents**? ❑Yes ❑No
   If no, where did you purchase this book? _____

   _____

3. What influenced your decision to purchase this book? (Check those that apply.)

❑ Cover	❑ Back cover copy
❑ Title	❑ Friends
❑ Publicity	❑ Other_____

4. How would you rate, on a scale from 1 (poor) to 5 (superior), the cover design? _____

5. On a scale from 1 (poor) to 10 (superior), please rate the following elements.

___Heroine   ___Plot

___Hero   ___Inspirational theme

___Setting   ___Secondary characters

6. What settings would you like to see covered in **Heartsong Presents** books?_____

_____

_____

7. What are some inspirational themes you would like to see treated in future books?_____

_____

_____

8. Would you be interested in reading other **Heartsong Presents** titles? ❑ Yes   ❑ No

9. Please check your age range:
   ❑ Under 18   ❑ 18-24   ❑ 25-34
   ❑ 35-45   ❑ 46-55   ❑ Over 55

10. How many hours per week do you read? _____

Name _____

Occupation _____

Address _____

City_____ State_____ Zip _____

······Hearts♥ng ······

HEARTSONG PRESENTS TITLES AVAILABLE NOW:

Hearts♥ng Presents
Love Stories Are Rated G!

That's for godly, gratifying, and of course, great! If you love a thrilling love story, but don't appreciate the sordidness of some popular paperback romances, **Heartsong Presents** is for you. In fact, **Heartsong Presents** is the *only inspirational romance book club*, the only one featuring love stories where Christian faith is the primary ingredient in a marriage relationship.

Sign up today to receive your first set of four, never before published Christian romances. Send no money now; you will receive a bill with the first shipment. You may cancel at any time without obligation, and if you aren't completely satisfied with any selection, you may return the books for an immediate refund!

Imagine. . .four new romances every four weeks—two historical, two contemporary—with men and women like you who long to meet the one God has chosen as the love of their lives. . .all for the low price of $9.97 postpaid.

To join, simply complete the coupon below and mail to the address provided. **Heartsong Presents** romances are rated G for another reason: They'll arrive *Godspeed!*